T0017283

If I Were the Ocean,
I'd Carry You Home

If I Were the Ocean,
I'd Carry You Home

STORIES

PETE HSU

2020
Red Hen Press
Fiction Award

Red Hen Press | *Pasadena, CA*

Book design by Mark E. Cull

Names: Hsu, Pete, 1972– author.
Title: If I were the ocean, I'd carry you home: stories / Peter Hsu.
Other titles: If I were the ocean, I'd carry you home (Compilation)
Description: First edition. | Pasadena, CA: Red Hen Press, [2022] | "2020
    Red Hen Press Fiction Award."
Identifiers: LCCN 2022007381 | ISBN 9781636280530 (paperback) | ISBN
    9781636280547 (ebook)
Subjects: LCGFT: Short stories.
Classification: LCC PS3608.S885 I38 2022 |
    DDC 813/.6—dc23/eng/20220302
LC record available at https://lccn.loc.gov/2022007381

The National Endowment for the Arts, the Los Angeles County Arts Commission, the Ahmanson Foundation, the Dwight Stuart Youth Fund, the Max Factor Family Foundation, the Pasadena Tournament of Roses Foundation, the Pasadena Arts & Culture Commission and the City of Pasadena Cultural Affairs Division, the City of Los Angeles Department of Cultural Affairs, the Audrey & Sydney Irmas Charitable Foundation, the Kinder Morgan Foundation, the Meta & George Rosenberg Foundation, the Albert and Elaine Borchard Foundation, the Adams Family Foundation, the Riordan Foundation, Amazon Literary Partnership, the Sam Francis Foundation, and the Mara W. Breech Foundation partially support Red Hen Press.

First Edition
Published by Red Hen Press
www.redhen.org

ACKNOWLEDGMENTS

The following stories have previously appeared in these respective publications:

The Bare Life Review: "Korean Jesus"; *The Best of* It's 5 O'Clock Somewhere: "The Donkey Is Definitely Asian"; *Faultline*: "Pluto"; *The Los Angeles Review*: "From the Brush, A Frantic Rustling" (as "Pieces"); *The Margins*: "A Penny Short"; *Pinball*: "King Kong Korab" (as "The Gift"); *Saga*: "Astronauts"; *Two Hawks Quarterly*: "If I Were the Ocean, I'd Carry You Home" (as "Chengdu"); and *Your Impossible Voice*: "There Are No More Secrets on Planet Earth."

This collection owes a debt to the vibrant and generous spirit of the Los Angeles writing community of which the following played particularly important roles:

Red Hen Press, The Red Hen Fiction Prize, and *The Los Angeles Review*: Dr. Kate Gale, Tobi Harper, Monica Fernandez, Rebeccah Sanhueza, Tansica Sunkamaneevongse, and Susan Straight

Those who have given my stories a home on stage, online, or in print: Alistair McCartney, Anelise Chen, Cassie Leone, Charles Jensen, Conrad Romo, Dani Hedlund, David Pischke, Deborah Lott, J. Ryan Stradal and Summer Block, Jason Casem, Jim Ruland, Joe O'Brien, Julia Ingalls, Keith Powell, Lily Anne Harrison, Lisa Teasley, Liv Vordenberg, Lucas Church, Maria Kuznetsova, Michele Raphael and David Lott, Michelle Franke, and Umi Hsu

My community at large: Alex Espinoza, Amanda Fletcher, Angus McNair, Anthony Garcia, Ashaki Jackson, Ben Loory, Brad Listi, Brooke Delaney, Charles Yu, Chelsea Sutton, Chiwan Choi, Chris Daley, Chris Lee, Chris Terry,

Dave Thomas, David Francis, Don Martinez, Elliott Chen, F. Douglas Brown, Jade Chang, Janet Fitch, Jenn Dees, Jian Huang, Joseph Tepperman, Julia Callahan, Leslie Schwartz, Lindsey Styrwoll, Luis J. Rodriguez, Luis Romero, Marnie Goodfriend, Maeve Bowman, Meg Howrey, Mike Buckley, Mira Velimirovic, Miwa Messer, Natalie Chudnovsky, Natalie Green, Natalie Lima, Natashia Deón, Noel Alumit, Patrick O'Neil, Paul Mandelbaum, Sam Dunn, Steph Cha, Tony DuShane, and so many others, most especially: Breanna Chia, Heather Chapman, Jessica Shoemaker, Chinyere Nwodim, Kirin Khan, Soleil David, Greg King, Hyunsoo Moon, David Huang, Daniel Yang, Evan Chan, and J. Ryan Stradal

And my family: Carol Tai Au, John Au, Dan Hsu, Rebecca Au Williams, and all my Hsu's, Au's, Tai's, Williams's, Chou's, Concepcion's, Wu's, Shin's, Chi's, and Yoo's

And my most dear: Jacob, Rainer, Helen

for Helen

Contents

If I Were the Ocean,
I'd Carry You Home

Part One

PLUTO

It was exactly one year ago that Mom died. I know now they call that a deathday, but back then we didn't have a word for it. We didn't have a word for it, so maybe that's why nobody mentioned it. Not me or Dad or my brothers or my little sister either. Instead it seemed like a regular summer day. Us kids were still out of school for vacation, and Dad hadn't been working for the past couple weeks. We were all five of us in the apartment together: me and Dad, my older brothers Stevie and Clayton, and our littler sister Maddy. We were all in the living room where the big AC was. We had it on full, but it was still hot. The heat made the apartment feel really crowded, which was okay by me, but not so much for Dad and Stevie. Dad seemed frustrated with not getting any peace, not getting any quiet. Stevie seemed frustrated with having to take care of us littler ones. The two of them both seemed frustrated with each other, as if the apartment was a wild west town that wasn't big enough for the both of them.

Stevie wanted to go see *The Exorcist* at the Edwards, but Dad wouldn't take us.

Stevie said, "You gotta be kidding me."

Dad said, "It's too scary for the others."

Us three boys had already seen it, so Stevie said, "We've already seen it."

Dad said, "Not Maddy. Not Paul."

Stevie said, "Paul's seen it," and he pointed at me. I nodded and said that I saw it. Dad sighed really hard and rubbed his face, "We don't have money for the movies."

Then he sort of called out to us all. We got around him, and he told us that we all needed to get outside.

He took us out to the city college stadium. It was around six o'clock and still really hot when we got there. We stood around a minute while Dad did stretches. Then Stevie and Clayton said they wanted to play football. Dad said he was gonna go jogging. Maddy then said she also wanted to play football too. Dad told them all that was fine and then looked at me. I would have rather played football too, but it seemed like Dad wanted me to jog with him. He didn't actually say that, but it's what I thought he wanted.

So, me and Dad got on the track while Stevie and Maddy went out onto the field. Clayton went back to the truck to get the football. Then they were all three playing, Maddy looking tiny out there as she ran across the field and yelled for the ball. Clayton threw it. He threw it hard, but Maddy still caught it.

"Atta girl!" said Clayton.

Then Stevie raised his hand and said, "Give it here."

Maddy threw the ball to Stevie. It was a clumsy throw. Stevie had to take a couple steps up to get it. He then held the ball in one hand and lined Clayton and Maddy up in formation, Clayton at receiver and Maddy on defense. Stevie got into a quarterback crouch and said, "Hut, hut, hut, go," and Clayton started running. It was an easy route, just a straight run up the sideline. Stevie let Clayton get up the field. Maddy ran behind him, almost ten yards back. Stevie waited a couple seconds, then he let the ball go and it was like a kind of throw like from a movie, spinning through the air in a rainbow arc, sunlight glinting off the laces.

The ball hit Clayton in the palms of his open hands. He grabbed it and then slowed down to let Maddy catch up. Maddy jumped on his leg. He then started running again, with her still holding on to him. The three of them looked like they could have done that all day. Stevie calling out routes, Clayton and Maddy taking turns at receiver.

Meanwhile, Dad and I ran the track. Nobody to chase. Nobody to be chased by. No routes except the steady orbit of the four-hundred-meter loop, counter-clockwise, over and over and over, tracking every lap, every lap a quarter mile, every four laps a mile.

Dad said, "We're gonna do two and a quarter today," and I knew that meant two and one quarter miles, which meant nine laps. There were nine lanes on the track, which meant that we could do one lap in each lane. So, if we started in lane one, we would finish in lane nine. On the first lap, I didn't say anything. Dad didn't either. I didn't like to initiate conversation. But Dad usually talked a lot, so it was uncomfortable to just be jogging in silence. We stayed quiet until we crossed the line with the lane number painted on to it. I called off one of the planets. The first one.

I said, "Lane one, Mercury."

Dad looked at me like he thought I was weird. Then we

went back to jogging, and at the end of the next lap, I did the same thing with the second planet, and then the next, and the one after that:

I said, "Lane two, Venus."

I said, "Lane three, Earth."

I said, "Lane four, Mars."

At Mars, Dad asked about school.

I said, "It's summer. There's no school."

Dad said, "I mean in a general kind of way."

I said, "I don't know, I guess it's fine."

Dad said, "Fine?"

I didn't say anything to that.

Dad said, "How did that planets stuff go?"

The past year I had a planets project where I had to make a travel brochure for one of the planets. I did mine on Pluto. I didn't pick Pluto. We just had them assigned to us.

"So," said Dad, "a travel brochure for Pluto? Jesus, it must be freezing on Pluto. That's the first thing, the cold. How about that?"

I hadn't thought about it being cold there.

I said, "I made it a memorial kind of place, like for people to visit or something."

Dad said, "Like a cemetery."

"No. It's not for burying the bodies. The dead people's, like, spirits would still be there."

"Like heaven."

"Sort of, but not like a happy place. Everybody sort of floats around like a zombie there."

"So, like hell then."

"No, not like a punishment."

Then Dad said he didn't get it, and I tried to explain how Pluto is sort of the prison guard of dead people, keeping them from breaking out and alive people from breaking in. I tried to explain this, but I was out of breath and my stomach hurt, so I stopped talking. Dad also wasn't talking. He was just jogging, and I thought maybe he was thinking about Pluto and cemeteries and dead people, and then thinking about Mom. I thought maybe that was what he thinking about and that was why he wasn't talking.

Then he started talking again.

He said, "I don't get the mythology stuff. Wasn't this supposed to be for science?"

I said, "I don't know."

Dad said, "Okay."

We kept jogging.

I said, "Lane five, Jupiter."

I said, "Lane six, Saturn."

I said, "Lane seven, Uranus."

I looked over to Stevie and Clayton and Maddy. Maddy had the ball. She held it with two hands, over her head. It looked three times bigger than her head. Stevie pretended to chase her, running around her in circles. Maddy screamed. Clayton ran around Maddy too, in the same direction, and shouted, "Throw it, Maddy! Throw it!"

Maddy said, "Okay!"

Clayton said, "Throw it!"

Maddy said, "Okay!"

Then she pulled the ball back and threw it. She threw it and it looked like it was going to go really far, except it was off course. It was going away from Stevie and Clayton and toward the track. Stevie and Clayton started cheering and running toward where Maddy threw the ball. The ball was heading right toward me and Dad. It got to us and hit the ground and rolled around some. I just ignored it, but Dad slowed down and picked it up. He picked it up and held it for a second. He held it and looked at Maddy and Clayton and Stevie. He kind of patted the ball with his hand and then threw it to Stevie. He threw it really hard and fast and it looked like a real football throw. It looked like a real football throw, like how Stevie throws. I'd never seen him do that before. Stevie caught the ball and kind of looked at Dad like he was also impressed.

Dad said, "Nice catch." And then he started walking toward Stevie. As he was walking toward Stevie, Stevie threw the ball back at Dad. Dad stuck out one hand and sort of snatched it out of the air.

Clayton said, "Whoa!"

Maddy said, "Whoa!"

Stevie didn't say whoa, but he did clap his hands together like he was excited. Dad laughed and threw the ball to Clayton, who caught it regular with both hands. Then they passed it back and forth, and then started a game. It was more like a real game because there were four of them now, even if Maddy was little.

I kept jogging. I'm pretty sure they would've let me play too. But I didn't go play with them. I kept jogging the laps. I jogged the next lap which was lane eight, Neptune. I then came up on the next lap which was lane nine, which was Pluto. So, I jogged lane nine and watched them play. Maddy had the ball again. She didn't throw it. She stood there and kept screaming. Stevie kept running. Clayton kept running. Dad kept running. And I also kept running. I kept running and maybe that would have been a good time to think about things. I could have thought about Pluto. I could have thought about the spirits of the dead floating around like zombies forever. Maybe I could have thought about Mom. But I didn't think about Mom. I didn't think about Pluto. I didn't think about anything. I just ran. I ran lane nine again. And when I finished that lap, I ran lane nine again. And then again. Around and around and around.

KING KONG KORAB

Grandpa Marvin put The Enforcer in park and turned around to talk to the two young boys in the backseat. The older one was Reggie. He was nine, but big for his age. The little one was Max, and he was still only five. He had his hair long. It was in his eyes. He was wearing a yellow T-shirt with a purple number sixteen on the back. That shirt used to be Reggie's before Reggie got chubby and his clothes wouldn't fit anymore.

"Reggie, Max," said Marvin. "You see that man in the Jeep? Honks at me and then runs away. Is that how men do things?"

The two boys both replied with an enthusiastic, "No!"

Marvin said, "Good boys," and then reached back and tousled Max's hair. It flung back and forth. Max looked up at him. He giggled. He was a nice kid. Marvin babied him. Max wanted a kitten; they got a kitten. Max's favorite color was pink; no problem. Max wanted tumbling instead of hockey; well, that's where Marvin drew the line. Max could wear a pink jersey with Malibu Ken on the chest, as long as he laced 'em up and skated with the rest of them.

Marvin grabbed Max's shoulder and shook him gently. He looked at Reggie and winked.

"Okay, boys. Let's go. We're late. You boys have the gift?"

Reggie grabbed the birthday gift. It was a box about the size of a backpack. He shoved it into Max's arms.

He said, "Hold this."

Max wrapped his hands around it. He nodded.

Uncle Pete saw them out front. He wasn't their real uncle. He just worked the ports with Marvin. He waved them all over, and he and Marvin started talking hockey.

Marvin pointed at Max.

"The little one's a natural, great tools. Skate. Handle. He can shoot. He just needs a little, you know."

Marvin flexed his biceps and made a fake angry face.

Pete nodded and pointed at Reggie.

"That's what big brothers are for, right, Reggie?"

Reggie froze.

"I dunno."

Marvin jumped in.

"That's right. The fat one's clumsy, but he's tough, tough like Jerry Korab."

Pete said, "Fuckin' King Kong Korab?"

Reggie didn't like being compared to Jerry Korab, who was Marvin's hero. Marvin was excited because Jerry Korab got traded to the Kings. But Jerry Korab sucked.

Marvin looked at Reggie.

Reggie said, "Jerry Korab sucks."

Marvin laughed. He turned back to Pete.

Pete said, "It's true. Korab's just a goon."

Marvin crouched and put up his dukes like he and Pete were going to start boxing.

"Now, come on. Dave Schultz, Moose Dupont, those are goons. But Jerry Korab's better than that. Korab can play. But he'll sacrifice his stats to be Dionne's bodyguard, to make sure nobody bullies The Little Beaver."

Pete laughed, "The Little Beaver."

Marvin patted Pete on the back and directed him through the gate and toward the front door. They started to walk into the party, but Max had wandered off back into the street. Reggie saw him. He was peeking in from the gate. Reggie gave him a stern look. Max hurried back.

As they walked through the door, Genna, the birthday girl, walked up to the boys, standing what Reggie felt was too close. They all three stood there for about a second. Then Genna looked at her mom. Her mom nodded. Genna sighed and ran off to join the other kids.

Genna's mom was Mrs. Martinez. She was a teacher at Reggie and Max's school. She talked to them without looking at them.

"Hello, Reginald. Maxwell. Where's your father?"

Marvin was their grandfather, not their dad, but Max pointed to him anyway.

Mrs. Martinez said, "You can place your gifts on the table."

She motioned to a folding table. The table was covered in birthday presents. Reggie turned to Max. He was about to repeat the instructions when he saw that Max wasn't holding the gift.

"Where's the gift?"

Max didn't say anything. Reggie looked around.

"Where is it?"

"Someone said leave it outside."

"Well, go get it."

But Max wouldn't go. He shook his head. He folded his arms.

〜

Marvin and Reggie came back from outside the house. They'd looked all over the yard and street. They didn't find the gift. Marvin asked Max again about what happened. Max told Marvin the same thing that he told Reggie, that somebody said to leave the gift outside. Marvin looked at the two boys with his eyebrows scrunched up.

"What in the heck. Why would anybody tell you that?"

Max didn't answer. Marvin looked at him like he was about to get upset. Marvin then started asking Reggie questions. Reggie told him that he didn't have the gift, and that Max was the one in charge of it. Max started crying. Marvin stuck his finger in Reggie's chest.

"Don't be a snitch."

Reggie looked down and felt guilty. Marvin then squatted and focused his attention on Max. He went through the same questions: Who told you to leave the gift outside; was it a kid or a grown-up; did you see the person here, anywhere, at the party; was it somebody you knew or a stranger. He asked if it was a boy or a girl, a man or a woman, if they were friendly or mean, if they were Mexican or white or Black or Chinese or half, because there were some half kids at this party, or if they were tall or short, glasses or no-glasses, fat or skinny. At this last question Max finally answered.

Max said, "Fat."

Marvin stood up.

Marvin said, "Fat."

Marvin looked at Reggie. Reggie guessed because he was fat.

Reggie said, "It wasn't me."

Marvin frowned. Reggie didn't know if Marvin believed him. Then Marvin looked around the room. Reggie looked around too. There weren't any other fat people. Nobody else at the party was fat. They were either skinny or regular.

Marvin said, "Fat. Okay, that's something."

He looked at Max again. Max looked like he was gonna cry again. Marvin waved both hands in Max's face.

"No, no, no. It's okay. We'll find them. A fat person. Okay."

The Martinez house was really big. Marvin led the boys from room to room. They started with the kitchen. Marvin said that was the most logical because fat people like kitchens. They looked through the kitchen. It was as big as their apartment. There were a bunch of people. Mrs. Martinez was at the stovetop making something that smelled like carnival popcorn. Three men were at the bar drinking beer. People passed through while they watched. The people grabbed things and walked back out. They checked them all out. None of them were fat.

Marvin opened a beer. He took a long sip. He held the bottle to his mouth as he looked around. He took another sip and said, "Let's go."

The three of them walked out the backdoor. They walked into the backyard. There were no fat people back there either. People started to notice that they were up to something. Somebody asked Marvin what was wrong. Marvin said, "Nothing." But Reggie and Max could tell that he was starting to get frustrated.

Then he said, "What kind of creep would trick you kids like that? It's not even expensive stuff."

He started calling the person "the fatso." He looked at Reggie every time he said it.

They went back into the house. They searched the living room again. They checked the downstairs bathroom. They went into the game room. No luck.

Marvin took the boys upstairs. Max tried to tell him that Mrs. Martinez wouldn't like it if they went upstairs. Reggie told Max to shut up.

Marvin said, "It's okay. This is important."

The three of them went upstairs. They searched each room. They checked the closets. They checked behind the shower curtains. Marvin even looked under the beds and in the drawers. Nothing. They came back down. They stood in the living room.

Marvin said, "By now the fatso could've gone back into the kitchen or the backyard, and we wouldn't even know it."

They went through the kitchen again. They looked around as they walked. Then they were back in the backyard. They went through the side gate and out to the front yard. They looked around. There were also no fat people in the front yard.

Marvin said, "What the fuck, Max. Are you sure that's all you remember?"

Max looked at Reggie like he didn't know what to do. Reggie looked away. Marvin almost never cussed at them. Max started crying. Marvin lost his patience.

Marvin said, "Stop it. Stop. Crying's for babies. Are you a baby? No? Then stop crying right now."

This made Max cry more.

Reggie said, "Stop. Stop crying."

Marvin punched Reggie lightly in the stomach. Reggie was not sure why he did that. It hurt a little bit.

Reggie went back to looking for fat people. He saw this carnival picture booth in the corner with the curtain closed. He pointed at it. Marvin patted him on the back. Marvin and Reggie walked over. They stood in front of the curtain. They waited for a couple pictures and then the curtain opened. Inside were four kids. Reggie knew them from school. They were two grades older than Reggie. They were Rob Ridley, Bernie Vo, Luke Beauchamp, and Claude Hsieh. Rob, Bernie, and Luke were all regular size. Claude was fat. Marvin looked at Claude.

Marvin said, "Hey, fatso. Hold it right there."

Claude tried to run away, but Marvin grabbed him by the shirt collar and held him. The other three boys ran off.

Marvin said, "Not so fast. What's your name?"

Reggie answered before Claude could say anything. "Claude Hsieh."

Marvin said, "Claude Hsieh?"

He looked at Reggie. Reggie nodded. Marvin looked at Claude.

Marvin said, "Okay, Claude. Where is it?"

Claude said, "What?"

He looked scared.

Marvin said, "The gift. Where's my grandson's gift? What's going on here, some kind of prank?"

Claude said, "What?"

"Are you messing with me?"

"What? No?"

Claude looked at Reggie. His eyes were wide. Claude was a mean kid. He was a bully, especially to girls, especially if they were pretty or if they were nice.

Marvin said, "Listen, Claude. I know what you did, you little goon. I need the gift back. Right now. Give it back."

Claude looked at Marvin. He looked at Reggie. He looked back at Marvin.

Claude said, "What?"

Marvin said, "Kid, stop messing with me."

Marvin still had Claude by the collar. He held it pretty tight. Other adults started to notice what was happening. In a second or so, Mr. Hsieh came out to the front yard. He was shouting, "Hey. Let go of my kid!"

Marvin looked up.

"Now, hold on. Your kid stole our gift. I'm just trying to get it back."

"What? What the hell are you talking about? Claude?"

Claude looked at his father. He was talking in a whiny voice.

Claude said, "I didn't do anything."

Marvin and Mr. Hsieh started arguing.

Mr. Hsieh said, "Claude has nothing to do with this."

And then, Mr. Hsieh said, "I'm calling the cops if you don't let him go immediately."

Marvin said, "This fatso's a dirty thief."

Reggie was pretty sure that Mr. Hsieh was then about to punch Marvin, and that Marvin wanted Mr. Hsieh to punch him so that Marvin could start punching back because the truth was, even though Marvin was much older than Mr. Hsieh, Reggie knew that Marvin would beat Mr. Hsieh in a fight.

While this was going on, nobody, besides Reggie, noticed that Max had slipped away again. He walked out past the gate and out of sight. Then he came back. He was holding his hands behind his back. Reggie saw what he was holding. This confused Reggie for a second. Then he saw the look on Max's face and motioned for Max to get rid of it, but Max held on to it. He held on to it and walked up to Marvin. He was crying. It was the gift in his hands. It was torn open and stuffed back into its box. It was a purple dress and faux mink stole which was also dyed purple. He held the gift out to Marvin, still walking toward him. He was trying to talk through his crying.

He said, "I'm sorry."

Marvin was still holding Claude by the collar. He looked at Max with one eyebrow raised. Mr. Hsieh took Marvin's hand and removed it from Claude's shirt. He did this slowly. Marvin didn't seem to notice this happening. Once his hand was pulled off, Marvin turned to Mr. Hsieh like he was surprised to see him. Max was still standing there holding the dress.

Marvin said, "Buddy? What's going on? Did you find it?"

Max said, "I'm sorry. I kept it."

Then Claude smiled. He looked happy. He clapped his hands and started laughing. He pointed at Max. He shouted so loud the whole party could hear.

Claude said, "Look at the sissy! He wants to wear a dress! Sissy!"

Another kid started laughing. Then more. Boys and girls both laughed. Parents seemed to be trying to tell their kids to stop laughing. That only made them laugh harder. Rob Ridley, Bernie Vo, and Luke Beauchamp were all laughing. Genna Martinez was there. She was saying something like, "Oh, how cute," but she was still laughing. Some of the parents even started laughing. They were less loud. It was hard to tell if they meant to be mean or if they were just uncomfortable, but Reggie saw them. They were laughing. Mr. Hsieh, Mrs. Martinez, they were all laughing. Uncle Pete was there too. He wasn't laughing. He put a hand on Marvin's shoulder. He said something. Marvin looked at him. He looked around at everybody else. He saw them. He didn't laugh.

Marvin grabbed hold of Max, who was crying very hard by then. He picked him up. He held him in one arm. Max had his arms wrapped around Marvin's neck. He was saying sorry. He dropped the dress on the ground. Marvin stepped on it. It looked like that was by accident. Then Marvin carried Max past the other people. He carried him out toward the street. Uncle Pete walked after them but stopped once Marvin passed the front gate. Reggie started to follow. Claude came up beside him and said, "Your brother's a sissy."

Reggie turned to Claude. He looked Claude in the face. Claude looked like a real goon. He had a big stupid grin. His eyes were squinted shut from the laughing. Reggie looked at him, and he swears this is true. He wanted to punch Claude right in the mouth. He wanted to punch all those people right in the mouth. But he didn't. He turned to back to Claude. He laughed. He said, "What a sissy."

FROM THE BRUSH, A
FRANTIC RUSTLING

Penny Leong is eight years old and home by herself. At the kitchen table, she is playing at organizing a large extended family of toys, arranging them with the strong toys along a perimeter surrounding the gentle ones within it. As she plays, a loud knock from the front door startles her. She freezes, stopping in midmotion. She then slowly stretches out her hands across the table, hovering over the toys like a protective mother blanketing her children from harm. Just out of her reach is a Yellow Power Ranger action figure. The Yellow Ranger stands still. It is stationed on the furthest edge of the table, the strongest of Penny's toys.

The Yellow Ranger's form is feminine like a Barbie doll. It is dressed in a comic book superhero costume. It wears a mask. It holds a laser rifle. It is missing one leg. It is standing on its one remaining leg.

It starts to teeter. Penny shushes the Ranger.

"Stay still."

But it falls, and Penny gasps. Then, another knock at the door. Another gasp. Penny stumbles to her feet and then is still again. She places both hands over her mouth, and the knocking stops. She takes a deep breath and decides that, despite being scared, she should investigate. She exhales and makes her way to the front door, stepping only on the floorboards that don't squeak. At the door, she looks through the scratched and foggy peephole. The features of the person on the other side are blurred, but Penny can tell who it is by his bulk and his slouch.

It's Bobby. Bobby is her mother's ex-husband. Bobby is Penny's ex-stepfather.

Bobby says, "Lucky, I know you're there. I can see you through the peephole."

She thinks that he probably can't see her through the peephole, but she doesn't know this for certain. She ducks down. She puts her hands on the doorknob, not yet turning it. Bobby knocks again.

"Come on, girl. It's Bobby Baba. Open up."

"You're not my baba."

"Oh, come on."

Bobby laughs and holds up a large rectangular case.

He says, "Look here. I got something. I promise, you're gonna like it."

Penny looks again through the scope of the peephole. One eye closed. One eye open. She focuses between the scratchy lenses to find a small clear window. She looks at the case. It's long and black with chrome trim. On the front is a small brass plate bolted onto the black plastic. The plate has a lightning bolt on it. It looks like the Power Rangers logo. Penny knows Bobby used to be a kind of a ranger. He could have been a Power Ranger. But that's stupid. But still, maybe.

She turns the knob slightly. Bobby pushes through as soon

as there's give in the door. He does this with authority, but not violence. Penny is moved aside. Bobby walks in. As he passes, he pats her on the head.

"There we are, how's my Lucky Penny, huh?"

Her hair is messy, tied into two uneven pigtails. Bobby grabs one pigtail and tugs on it. Penny relaxes a little bit, remembering how kind he could sometimes be. He puts down the long, rectangular case and squats next to her. He looks at her and opens his arms. She hugs him. His shirt smells like dirt and cigarettes. His skin smells like beer.

Bobby lets Penny go and heads into the kitchen. He picks up a bowl of cereal. It is one of three that Penny has rationed for the day. He scoops two spoonfuls into his mouth. It crunches as he chews. Still holding the bowl, he rummages through the refrigerator. He complains that there isn't anything decent to drink, and then returns with a mostly empty two-liter bottle of store-brand diet cola and a mostly full bottle of Thomas Araby's London Dry Gin. The gin is kept in the freezer. It has frost on its label.

Bobby sits down at the dining table. He pushes aside Penny's toys. He puts the bottles and a plastic tumbler down next to the Yellow Ranger. Bobby picks the Ranger up, running his thumb over the female anatomy of the plastic figure. A bolt of protectiveness jolts Penny. She wants to rescue the toy. She wants to snatch the figure out of Bobby's hand. She doesn't do it. She is scared to provoke him. He looks up from the toy. He looks at Penny. He smiles, putting the figure down, carefully bending it at its one remaining knee, adjusting it so that it balances on its one remaining foot. He then fixes himself a gin and coke. He takes a sip.

"Bleh, tastes like shit."

He drinks the rest and then pours himself another.

Penny says, "Mama'll be back soon."

Bobby bobs his head in small circles. He starts talking in a sing-song voice.

"I don't think so, no, no, no. No, I don't think so."

Bobby grins and raises his eyebrows.

"Yes, she will," says Penny. "She'll be back very, very soon."

"Quit. No secrets between us. Or maybe she's got secrets from you. But Bobby Baba knows all."

Penny purses her lips, angry that she doesn't know how to respond to this, and afraid that it's true.

Bobby says, "Besides, I am not here for your mom. I am here for you."

He taps his forefinger on the table as he says this last part. I. Tap. Am. Tap. Here. Tap. For you. Tap. Tap. Tap.

Penny watches her toys jostle on the table with each tap, jarred as if caught in a tiny earthquake. At the last tap, the Yellow Ranger falls over. Penny reaches out and grabs it. As she clutches the toy, Bobby reaches out and holds tight to Penny's hand.

He says, "You still playing with dolls?"

As he holds her hand, Penny can feel the Yellow Ranger's pointy foot dig into her palm. Bobby shakes his head as if to clear his eyesight and then nods toward the case.

"I think it's time to grow up. Put aside childish things."

Bobby takes another moment to focus and then gets up to retrieve the case. He yanks it off the ground, flinging it through the air and then uses it to swipe everything off the table. The bottles, his cup, and all of Penny's toys. Everything lands onto the kitchen floor with a clatter. Bobby laughs and fumbles with the combinations on the case latches. He turns the wheels over and over. Penny is tentative, but she leans forward. She's still holding her toy in one hand, but places the other on Bobby's shoulder. He undoes that last latch. He throws up the case and says, "Voila!"

Penny crowds in, smushed into Bobby's side. She drops the action figure and places both hands on the edge of the case. Her eyes are open wide and her jaw slackens. Inside the case, surrounded by fitted green velvet, is a long, black rifle.

Penny nods and looks at Bobby.

"Wow."

"You like it," says Bobby. "Course you do."

"Mama won't like it."

"Well good thing she's not here then."

Penny takes a small step backwards, away from the rifle.

"Where did you get this?"

"Bought it."

Penny knows that this shouldn't be true. She knows Bobby isn't allowed to do certain things, like work in the casino or reenlist, or buy a gun.

He takes the rifle out. He now seems much more sober. His movements seem controlled and deliberate. He holds the rifle with his right hand, his palm on the grip, his forefinger resting on the outer rim of the trigger guard. Penny stares at the rifle. She takes in its insistent simplicity, so different from her toy guns that are ornamented with endless buttons and switches, lights and speakers, plugs and attachments. Bobby's rifle is smooth and clean and singular in purpose.

Bobby holds it out to her.

"Go on, girl. Take it. It's fine. It's not loaded."

She takes the rifle with both hands. From stock to barrel, it is just a tad shorter than she is. She seems to have a general sense of how to carry the rifle. She holds it with great balance, as if it is an extension of her arm. Bobby nudges her. She pulls the rifle up, resting the stock in the crook of her shoulder. Bobby starts to help her position it, but then stops.

"You done this before, Lucky?"

The rifle is light in her arms, far lighter than she would ever have imagined a real gun would weigh. She stares down the sight, closing one eye. Bobby places a hand on her shoulder.

"Both eyes open," he says. "You need to see everything."

Penny opens both eyes and adjusts her vision. She lines up the rear sight to the front. She aims at a stack of mail on the counter top and, in her imagination, fires the rifle. Pow. She aims across the living room at the record player. Pow. She aims at her music bag. Pow. Her mother's high-heeled cowboy boots. Pow. The upright fan. Pow. The dusty faux flowers. Pow. The cracked frame with the old picture of Bobby and her mother standing on the steps of a worn brick building, Bobby thin with crew-cut hair and a heather-gray *Army of One* T-shirt, Penny's mom young and clear-eyed and ready to make a difference in the world, the two of them still so dumb to the scales of fate and consequence.

Penny pulls the trigger. It's soft and doesn't click. But in her head, Pow. Pow. Pow.

Penny lowers the rifle and looks at Bobby.

Bobby says, "Better days, right, Lucky?"

He walks across the room and takes the picture off the wall. He opens the back of the frame and takes the photograph out, looking at it for what seems like a long time before easing it into his jacket pocket. He finishes the rest of his drink and claps his hands together.

"Get your coat," he says. "Let's go shoot."

～

Bobby has classical music on in his truck, the kind he always liked, the slow sad kind. He hums along as he drives out, out a long way. They go through the city and up into the mountains. They pass at least one shooting range on the way. Penny can see the sign from the freeway. She asks why they don't go there, but Bobby brushes it off as: regulations. She asks him what that means. He says to her, "Rules, baby. Them's the rules."

They get into the winding switchbacks of the mountains. Bobby rolls down the windows. The air is cold and bites at the insides of Penny's nose. She takes a breath as big as she can. She exhales unevenly. She's afraid. She doesn't like this feeling of being afraid. It's confusing. She's not sure what she's afraid of. She is afraid of Bobby. But she's also glad to be with him. She's afraid of her mother. She's afraid that her mother will be angry with her when she finds out she went with Bobby. She's also afraid her mother will be sad and that Penny will feel like that is her fault, that her mother's sadness is her fault. She closes her eyes. The sadness seeps into her. She doesn't resist. Her head feels heavy. She lays her head down in Bobby's lap. As she starts to fall asleep she says in a voice that is not audible in the noisy cab of the truck, "Night night, Baba."

Bobby says, "Wakey, wakey. We're here."

Penny is already half-awake when she hears his voice. She pops up and flings open the door to Bobby's pickup truck. They're parked in a dirt clearing. There aren't any other cars. There are tall pine trees and large boulders in the distance. Closer is a fallen tree trunk. Bobby is opening the gun case and taking out the rifle. He removes the bolt from the rifle and looks down the bore and then through the open sights and then through the bore and then the sights again. He makes adjustments in between views. He does this several times and then reinstalls the bolt and places the rifle back in the open case. He then begins filling the cartridge with rounds of .243. Bobby explains this caliber is light enough for a child to handle, but strong enough to bring down a deer with a single shot. An important feature, he insists, so that the wounded animal doesn't run off into the woods to bleed out over the course of hours, or worse, to be maimed but not killed, becoming some kind of aberration, ostracized, starving and alone.

"Decisive," he says.

There's a brightness in his voice.

"Like flipping a switch. No questions. No take-backs. No negotiations. No hesitations, consultations, or explanations. Just wham, bam, thank you ma'am."

Bobby seems sober now, as if the drive and the fresh air rejuvenated him. But he's brought the bottle of Araby's. It protrudes from his back pocket. Bobby inserts the cartridge and shoulders the rifle. He takes a plastic garbage bag full of recyclables. Penny recognizes the bag from the apartment.

Bobby walks into the distance, toward the fallen pine tree. There he arranges cans and bottles along the top of it. He puts up five targets, one for each round in the magazine. He drops the bag with the remaining targets. He walks back to Penny with a spring in his step, holding the rifle out in front of him like a dance partner.

Penny remembers Bobby arguing with her mother about guns. There had been a shooting three cities over. Bobby had been drunk and in tears watching the television reports of children being gunned down in a cafeteria. He'd said that those poor little bastards hadn't had a chance. Bobby wanted to buy a gun in case anything like that happened around them. Her mother said it wasn't a good idea. Bobby said they needed protection. He said the world was gone to shit. Her mother called him a drunk and an idiot. Bobby warned her to not antagonize him. She said she wasn't. Bobby said she was, she always was.

Penny had then changed the television channel. She didn't know why she changed the channel, but she knew right away that she should not have. Bobby yelled at her because wasn't it obvious that he was still watching that. She tried to change it back, but the button didn't work. Bobby kicked a hole in the wall. Penny's mother yelled at Bobby to leave Penny alone. Bobby knocked her mother down. Penny ran and hid in her room, in the dark, in the corner of her closet. She thought about the kids who'd been shot.

"Okay," says Bobby. "This is twenty-five yards."

He scrapes the ground with the heel of his shoe.

"Follow me."

Penny follows him to the next marker.

He says, "Now, this is fifteen."

Then to the next.

"This is ten."

With that, Bobby pivots on his heel, pulling the rifle up to his shoulder as he does. He lands on both feet, turning to face the targets. He fires in one fluid motion. The rifle cracks with a loud pop. Penny covers her ears and closes her eyes. When she opens them, she sees Bobby. He is frowning.

"Shit. Missed."

He takes the rifle up again. He steadies himself. He takes his time to line up this next shot. Penny can hear him breathing. He inhales a gulp of air. He exhales. He pulls the trigger. He misses again. He looks as if he's surprised.

"Holy fuck, man. Hold on. One more."

He tries again. He misses again. He props the rifle against his leg and takes the bottle of Araby's from his pants pocket. He uncorks it and takes a steady sip. He wipes his mouth with his sleeve. As he puts the bottle back, he picks up the rifle and hands it to Penny.

"Whattaya say, Lucky? Give it a shot?"

Penny takes the rifle. She lowers it, barrel pointing to the ground. She places her right hand on the small metal ball of the bolt, lifts it and pulls a round into the chamber. She brings the rifle back up, up to the crook of her shoulder, like she did at the apartment. She does this with quiet seriousness. Bobby doesn't need to warn her not to point that thing at him or to keep her finger off the trigger until she's ready to shoot. It's as if she knows these things already. He helps her with her stance. With a couple of taps on her feet, she balances her weight and levels the rifle steady, its twenty-two-inch barrel parallel with the Earth. He stands behind her. He tells her to brace herself against him. She leans on his hip.

"Try to stay loose," he tells her. "This shit's gonna kick."

Penny fixes her eyes on the fallen trunk. She thinks about which target she wants to shoot. Roving from can to bottle to another can. She imagines the cans and bottles as the man who had shot up that school. She imagines him lurking in the distance, advancing on her and the other children. She imagines him close, very close, at the front doors. He doesn't see her, but she sees him. She looks into the face of her adversary. There you are. She takes in an even breath and pulls the trigger. There's a flash in her retina, a hard pop into her shoulder. A tin can explodes.

"Holy shit!" says Bobby. "Oh my God, Lucky, you did it! Try again!"

Penny doesn't answer to Bobby's praise. She cocks the rifle and braces herself against his leg again. She aims and fires. The wine bottle shatters. Bobby taps her shoulder and motions for the rifle. She gives it to Bobby. He reloads the cartridge. He does this quickly. He hands the rifle back to her.

"Okay, baby girl. Back up to the fifteen."

She backs up. He follows but stands a bit away.

"Now, you don't need me. Go on. Do it."

She does. She fires. Her small frame adapts quickly and absorbs the kick without fanfare. Over on the log, the soda can is knocked off. She continues: a blue bottle, a row of three empty beer cans. Bam. Bam. Bam. Bobby applauds after each. When they're all knocked off, he hurries back to the log and puts more targets up. She hits them all. He reloads the rifle and again sets up more targets. He calls out each, left, middle, left, right, last one. She hits each, on demand, as called. They move back to the twenty-five-yard mark. He calls out the targets again. She hits them all again.

Bobby is beside himself.

"A natural! You are a bona fide natural! Goddammit, I gotta take your ass to the county fair."

He continues to drink from the bottle of Araby's, but it still looks halfway full. He laughs and hugs Penny. She doesn't hug him back. She can feel the ache in her shoulder and the fatigue in her arms and her legs. But she doesn't want to stop.

Bobby loses his balance. He falls to the ground. He pulls Penny down next to him. He says, "Why, you," and tickles her. She's not ticklish. He stops. They lie on their sides, facing each other. She looks at Bobby. His hair is in his eyes. He is smiling and looking back at her, staring really.

"You're really beautiful, Lucky. You know that?"

She looks away, neither glad nor embarrassed.

"For real. You are. Jesus, I wish I could see you grown up."

"I'll be grown up soon."

"Yeah, but if your mama has her way, I won't be around to see it."

Penny looks at him, studying his face. His smile fades and his eyes drop.

She asks, "Why?"

But she already knows why.

Bobby says, "I'm sorry, baby. But she's right. I'm no good for you. I haven't been good. I haven't been around when you all needed me. You did need me. You needed somebody to look after you. Keep you safe."

Penny doesn't respond. She thinks about being safe. She's surprised at how odd that word lands on her mind. Like a strange leaf from a strange tree from a very far-away place.

Bobby reaches over and brushes the back of his hand against Penny's cheek. Penny flinches just a little bit. Bobby puts his hand at the back of her neck. She pulls away, scrambling to get her footing.

"Hey. Whoa, Lucky."

He sits up fast. He holds his hands out.

"Whoa. What's happening, kid? I'm not gonna hurt you. I wouldn't ever hurt you."

Penny backs up, looking at the rifle, propped up next to them against the fallen trunk.

"Come on, Lucky. Don't be mad at me."

"I'm not mad."

She turns and looks at the rifle again. Bobby watches her. She wonders if she can reach it before he can stop her.

"What are you thinking, Lucky? What's in that head of yours?"

"Nothing."

"Nothing?"

"Nothing."

"Okay," says Bobby. "Okay, now come on."

He holds his hands still up and open.

"You want to be the hunter now, little miss Earn'st Hemingway? You want to hunt? What do you say I take you on safari?"

The idea attracts Penny's attention. Bobby gets on to his feet and tucks the bottle away. He picks up the rifle and holds it out to her. She takes it.

Bobby says, "I didn't mean nothing."

He adjusts the rifle strap on Penny's shoulder. She nods. They go forward into the woods.

Every few minutes Bobby stops and makes a show of tracking something. He picks up a broken twig or sniffs at brush or checks out what might be a paw print in the mud. Each time he finds a clue, he takes a slow and focused sip from the bottle and, with dramatic seriousness, waves his hand at Penny and points forward, deeper into the trees.

Some short time later, Bobby and Penny come into a grassy clearing in between a stretch of brush and an array of big southern live oak trees. Bobby drops onto the ground, flat on his back. He stares up into the atmosphere. It's close to dusk. The sun is still lighting up the sky in a full blue, but the shadows are long. The temperature is starting to drop. Penny lays down next to him. She can smell his sour sweat along with the clean smell of the gin. He rolls onto his stomach and puts an arm over her.

"Jesus, Lucky. I think I'm drunk."

Penny lets the weight of his arm settle. It's heavy. It crushes her a little bit. But she doesn't mind it.

As she lies beside him, Penny sees something. It's in the distance, a small, stout figure. She pulls away from the crook of Bobby's elbow. She sits up cross-legged. She takes the rifle off her shoulder. Bobby turns to look in the direction Penny is looking.

"What is it, Lucky?"

She points to the brush, to a large oak out in front of it. The tree's trunk looks as thick as Bobby's pickup. Seven large branches reach out and up from the base. A shadow the size of a large dog moves slowly in front.

"Oh dang, a bear cub," says Bobby. "What the hell's she doing out here?"

Penny lifts the rifle to her shoulder. She bows her back to hunch over the sights. She aims at the baby bear. Bobby grabs her leg.

"Lucky, wait. Wait."

Penny steadies herself. She hears Bobby but doesn't lower the rifle. She sees the cub's face. She lines up the front sight with the rear, aiming at the animal's forehead. She inhales and rubs the trigger guard with the pad of her forefinger.

Bobby pats her on the leg.

"Lucky, wait."

She exhales, keeping the rifle steady.

Still on his stomach, Bobby eases himself up onto one elbow.

He says, "Now look. You cannot shoot that cub."

Penny says, "Why?"

"Because it's wrong, baby girl. That cub's just a kid, like you."

Penny thinks for a second.

Penny says, "But that doesn't matter. That cub's a bear. Bears are dangerous. They kill people. We need to stop them."

Bobby says, "Well, now. Maybe. But there's something else."

Penny takes one eye off the sights and looks to Bobby.

Bobby says, "That cub, she's supposed to stay there by that tree, close. The tree's supposed to be her sitter."

Penny says, "Bear cubs have babysitters?"

"Well, yes they do. Their mothers leave them by these trees."

Bobby's voice drops.

"But I'm telling you, kiddo. You fire that gun, that mother bear's gonna be on us quick. Maybe we'll have five minutes. But maybe we won't have even one. And an angry mother bear, shit, girl, you can pump that Remington empty into her, and she'd still tear us both to pieces."

Penny says, "I'm not afraid."

She pulls the bolt, bringing a new round into the chamber.

Bobby says, "It's not about being afraid, Lucky."

But no, she thinks. It is about being afraid.

Bobby scoots a little further back. He places one hand softly on the top of the rifle, over the barrel, covering the rear sight.

Bobby says, "You gotta trust me on this, kid. A mother bear's not fucking around when it comes to her babies."

Penny stares through Bobby's hand. She can see a line from the rifle's sights across the field and into the cub. The line is clear, as if drawn with a ruler across a long sheet of vellum. She thinks about the mother bear. Imagines it. Covered in bristled fur and thick sinewy muscle. Penny imagines it standing tall on its hind legs. It towers over Penny and over Bobby too. It towers over the trees, over the mountains, over the Earth itself. Penny imagines it snarling, its teeth long and sharp with foamy spit dripping off. She imagines the growling. The growling like a language. It is a language that she and her mother and Bobby too, would know. The language of the strong directed at the weak. The language that burrows into the skulls of the vulnerable, echoing against the shone alabaster walls of dark closets and shut eyes. Penny moves her forefinger from the guard onto the trigger.

Bobby says, "Hey, hey."

He keeps his hand laid on top of the rifle.

"Come on, girl."

She blinks. Tears welled in her eyes drop onto her cheeks.

"No," she says.

"Lucky, whatever you're thinking."

Penny squeezes the trigger. The rifle fires. Bobby screams. He takes his hand from the barrel. In the distance the bear cub falls. Penny rises to her feet. She reloads the rifle. From the brush, a frantic rustling.

GAME FIVE

Game One: Sunday, June 2, 1991. The Los Angeles Lakers steal home-court advantage, beating the Bulls in Chicago. Unlikely hero Sam Perkins gives the Lakers the deciding lead with a 3-point make at fourteen seconds on the clock. Bulls star Michael Jordan takes the game's final shot, which rattles in-and-out of the rim as time expires. Final Score: Lakers 93–Bulls 91.

When our father moves back to Taiwan, he leaves John in charge. He gives him a list of rules for how to take care of me. The list covers school, money, girls, sports, and religion, and also stuff like hygiene and cooking. John says that it's too long. Our father says that John could do with following these rules himself. Then they argue, John's main point being that our father should stay if he's this concerned, and then our father's main point being that we should be grateful he didn't just disappear in the middle of the night like Cho Yuan's father. They go on like this for what seems like a long time. When they finish, they both have the same neutral expression on their faces, so it's hard to tell who won the fight. But the new list, it has only three rules: 1) do your homework;

2) go to church every Sunday; 3) watch all Lakers games. Our father says that he is confident that if we follow these three instructions, I'll turn out okay. Then he and John shake hands.

Over the next three years, John holds steady. Every day, "You done your homework?" All through spring, "Hey, Lakers tonight." And every Sunday, "Get up, Chris, we're late."

The church we go to is our father's old church, a Taiwanese church in Chatsworth. We go to the English service, which starts after the Taiwanese service, but still, we're never on time. On the day of Game One, John circles the parking lot, looking for a space. We can hear the church band from outside. They're like a rock band, like the kind that's popular in those days, nostalgic, even when it's new.

We end up parking on the curb, and come in through the back. The band's in the middle of an upbeat song. The drummer's this white guy called Woods. He plays too fast. The rest of the band struggles to keep up. The words to the song are up on a projector screen. The people in the front sing along and sway, their hands up in the air. I sometimes want to do that too, but I'm too embarrassed. I just clap, or more usually stand with my hands in my pockets.

Off the stage and to the side is the new pastor, our cousin, Cho Yuan. Cho nods at John. John does not acknowledge him, but I wave. Cho points at me and yells out, "AC Green in the house," loud enough for everyone to hear.

John and I sit in the back. Most of the rest of the audience is up close to the front. We also used to sit in the front, but these days John says he likes it in the back. He says, "That's where Jesus would sit," which sounds like a joke, but I know he's being serious.

With the music still going, Cho steps onto the stage. Bible in one hand, ragged and bent, with paper scraps sticking out of it. He slaps it against his hip like a tambourine. The band slows down and goes into a kind of instrumental bridge. Cho speaks into the microphone, "Lord bless the words of this humble servant." Then, he puts the Bible down on the podium and goes into a long discussion of the NBA Finals.

Cho says, "Who here's watching Game One today?"

Most of the kids raise their hands. A couple of the boys shout out, "Go Lakers!" Then John joins in, his voice deep and booming, "Bulls suck!"

Cho laughs and puts his hands up, "Now, now. Let's remember to be kind to any Chicagoans in the house." By which Cho means himself. He was born in Chicago and calls himself a Chicagoan, even though he's lived in Reseda since he was ten. For sports, he still roots for the Bears and the Blackhawks, but had been a Lakers fan until recently when the Bulls got good.

Cho makes a performance of checking his watch. The boys are still horsing around. Cho says, "Ok, let's get this show started. We wouldn't want to miss the tip." A boy snickers and says, like as a question, "the tip," like it's some kind of penis joke. Then some other boys laugh and repeat, "the tip." Then John repeats the whole phrase, enunciating each word, "Wouldn't want to miss the tip." Cho looks at John. He shakes his head and rolls his eyes and then goes on with his sermon.

It wasn't that long ago that John and Cho were friends. Cho and Cho's father had moved to Reseda, into the same apartment building as us. John was still in high school, and Cho wasn't the pastor yet, just another kid. The two of them were always together, along with Cho's girlfriend, Margaret. Back then the three of them were like the Valley's biggest Lakers fans, especially Cho. His favorite guys were Magic Johnson and James Worthy. Cho liked to call John "Magic." Himself, he called "Worthy." He tried calling Margaret "Jeannie," after Jeannie Buss, daughter of the Lakers' owner, but that didn't stick.

The three of them used to study videotapes of games, stopping and rewinding plays, memorizing the steps and movements, even the facial expressions, of the players. Once they broke it down, they'd go outside, John and Cho in jerseys, Margaret with the Camcorder, and they'd record themselves doing the plays. The three of them would then take those tapes into the AV room and edit them into their own personal highlight reels. The tapes got popular at church. Cho got more kids involved. They made copies of the tapes and passed them around. Margaret called it The Poseur's Comp. Eventually, I wanted to be in it too. Cho pointed at me and said, "Who do you want to be?"

I said that I didn't know, and then Margaret said, "How about Rambis?" She then flexed her biceps and winked at me.

"No," said John. "Not Rambis. Come on."

He punched me in the arm. I winced, and that seemed proof enough that I wasn't tough enough to be Kurt Rambis.

John said, "What about AC?"

"Yeah! Yeah, Chris will be AC," said Cho. "You know AC Green, right, Chris? A man of God, that guy."

Margaret said, "Guys, come on." She said that as if it wasn't cool for them to call me AC. I was only nine. I didn't know any better at the time. I was just happy to be a part of it. But before I knew it, every kid at church was calling me Virgo, because AC Green was more famous for being a virgin than for playing basketball. John and Cho confirmed that AC was a proud celibate, saving himself for marriage. I asked them if I could be some other player. Margaret said, "Maybe it's been going on for long enough."

Cho said, "Naw, it's a good nickname, and anyway, people don't get to choose their own nicknames."

Margaret said, "Really? And who named you Worthy?"

Cho laughed and put his arm around my neck and pulled me close. They'd been playing ball. Cho was sweaty and stank so bad. He put his mouth right up to my ear and said, "Kiddo, it's no put down. You're AC because you're the good one, the best one. The pure of heart. When the Lord comes, He'll look at you and say, behold my servant Christopher, blameless and upright. And that's when you're gonna put in a good word for the rest of us, right?"

～

Game Two: Wednesday, June 5, 1991. Jordan and the Bulls make a statement. With Game One hero Sam Perkins in the lane, Jordan drives hard, switching his ball-hand in midair to avoid the block. He banks in the layup. Chicago Stadium erupts. Jordan pumps his fist in celebration. The Bulls go on to win by 21. Final Score: Bulls 107–Lakers 86.

On Wednesdays, John does this volunteer job where he drives around town and drops off food for sick people. I'm usually in school when he goes, but that day I ditch, and he brings me along. His route changes some each week. I don't know why for sure, but I think it might be because some of the people die. Or maybe some of them get better, but that doesn't seem like how it works. A few of the stops are regulars. John's gotten to know them. Even I know a few of them. There's an old Black guy named Thompson. He's got so many books; he's always trying to give some to us. There's another guy named Ralph who's got cats, and never wants to talk; we just ring the bell and leave the food. There's a couple guys like that. Then there's Serge.

Serge is John's friend from the old days. They met in a PE class at CSUN, John's first year. They used to go out to K-Town together. Serge was a fifth-year and was a kind of a mentor to John. He taught him a lot about how to party. Not just how to party, but how to meet people, how to be confident. Now, John's a fifth-year, and Serge lives all the way out in the Canyon. John sets up his route so that Serge'll be our last stop. That way we can hang out a little bit.

Serge says, "Dude, my chicken is ice cold."

John smiles and apologizes, putting the container in the microwave. He then gets beers from the fridge and together us three go out onto Serge's porch.

Serge has AIDS. He's had it for a while now. He was the first person we'd ever known to get it, and he's one of the main reasons John does the route.

Serge makes a promise, "Next time, I'll cook for you guys. Fucking kimchi jjigae, how about that?" John agrees. He tells Serge he'll bring the beer. Serge tells John that he'll bring the girls. Serge laughs because he's not really bringing any girls over. I used to think Serge was gay, even before he got sick. One time, John told Serge, "Christopher thinks you're gay." I thought Serge would be mad, but he wasn't. He smiled and said that he didn't discriminate on race, creed, or gender. He was equal opportunity.

Serge puts two cigarettes between his lips and lights them both at the same time. He gives one to John. I feel like telling John not to take it, but I don't. Then the two of them smoke and tell stories about the old days. Once in a while, John'll let me take a sip from his beer, and Serge will try to include me in the conversation. He says things like, "Someday, little man, you'll have better stories than ours. I mean it. And I don't mean just party stories. You're gonna be somebody."

Then Serge starts crying. John grabs hold of him and pulls him into a tight hug, each of them resting their chin on each other's shoulder. It's sweet and also funny because they both keep smoking the whole time.

John asks me if I want food. I had eaten Serge's chicken dinner, so I'm not hungry, but I tell John yes anyway, so that we can hang out longer. And he says that we'll get burritos then.

We drive back through traffic, back to Reseda and to this Mexican place called Melina's. I eat chips and salsa as John orders. He doesn't get burritos. He gets the steak plate, two of them, and also fries, taquitos, and sodas. That's a lot of food for the two of us. Then John says that we're bringing it to Margaret's. I haven't seen Margaret since her last day at church. I say, "Margaret's on your route now?"

John does a sort of half-laugh, "No, she's not on the route. We're just going as friends."

I say, "Oh."

Margaret is Cho's ex-girlfriend Margaret. She used to work with Cho at church, in the music ministry. She resigned a year ago, but had been sick for the whole year before that. The church said she had to focus on her health. They'd made it seem like it was Margaret's own idea.

After Serge, Margaret was the second person we knew to get HIV. It was supposed to be private, but her healthcare was through the church so they found out and pretty quickly everybody knew. Then some of the boys started making up stories about who all she'd had sex with, and all the ways that she liked it. Their nickname for her was AIDS Face. I know it was wrong, but I started calling her that too. I said it once in front of John and regretted it as soon as the words came out of my mouth. I expected John to kick my ass, but he didn't.

John says, "What, you don't believe in helping our friends?"

"No," I say. "I mean, of course I do. Just didn't know that you and Margaret were still friends."

John says, "Of course we are."

It's almost six when we get to Margaret's apartment. I hold the food in two big bags and the drinks in a cardboard box. John buzzes the intercom. It takes a long time for Margaret to answer, but John doesn't ring again. We wait. It's Cho's old apartment, where we all used to hang out, watching cable or playing cards, sometimes all night, then waking up in the morning to Cho and Margaret clanging pots and pans, making breakfast for all of us, and talking about an adventure for the day, something wholesome like hiking or rollerblades.

When we see her, it takes me a second to understand who it

is. Margaret had been athletic and outdoorsy before, but now she's pale and skinny. Kinda boney and puffy at the same time. There are little circles on her arm of small, purple pools. I had not realized that someone could get that sick that fast. I try not to stare, but I do look whenever I think she isn't looking.

We sit, and John puts the food out, family style, on top of the flattened bags. He gets a steak knife from the kitchen and cuts the steaks into strips. He puts it all out in a kind of a mini-buffet, but Margaret barely eats, picking up a few fries and dipping them in house dressing.

The game is on the television. I take a soda and sit on the papasan. John and Margaret are on the couch. During commercial breaks, instead of talking about basketball, they talk about CSUN, John's classes: Lit Survey, Research Methods, Identity. His grades are good. Margaret seems proud. Then they talk about Cho and how the church is doing. They talk about music ministry. They talk about the other young people, the kids who used to spend their weekends here in this apartment, some of whom might want to send Margaret their best wishes, but none have actually come to see her.

John says, "They're fucking hypocrites."

Margaret says, "It's not their fault. I know they care."

Margaret takes John's hand and they lace their fingers together. Their two hands look mismatched.

John says, "I don't get it."

Margaret says, "It's okay. Hey, it really is. God is good. He really is."

"I don't know."

"He is."

"I don't know."

Margaret leans close to John, nudging him to smile, but he doesn't smile. She says to him, "This is how it is. If you believe in God, you believe in all of Him, the good and the terrible. When He gives us love, it's easy and we want to snatch it up greedy, like dogs. But when He gives us pain, we also need to embrace it, hold it, appreciate it."

John shakes his head, "How can God be good?"

"That's not the right question. The question is how can we say we believe in God if we don't trust Him?" She runs her fingers through his longish hair, tucking it behind his ears, "My sweet boy. Make sure you're all right. You can't wait like I did."

I look away, turning back to the television just in time to see Jordan drive the lane on Perkins. He goes up with his stupid tongue out like he's gonna dunk. But Perkins is there to meet him. Then Jordan in midair switches hands and lays it in with his left. The crowd goes nuts. Jordan is pumping his fist. His teammates are all crowding into him to give him high fives. The score is 97 to 71. There's still seven minutes to go. I keep watching, doing the math in my head of how many possessions the Lakers need to come back.

⁓

Game Three: Friday, June 7, 1991. The third contest of the series is tied at the end of regulation, but in overtime, Jordan and the Bulls overwhelm the overmatched Lakers, pulling away easily. Final Score: Bulls 104–Lakers 96 (OT).

It's the last day of school, a half day. John's waiting for me when I get out. I ask if we can give my friends a ride, but John says that he has a doctor's appointment. We drive up to CSUN and park on the street and walk a block onto campus.

Student Health is a big boxy, brick building. We take the stairs down to Laboratory & X-ray, and John says for me to wait for him. He points at a row of blue vinyl chairs. I don't sit down. I ask him what we're doing there. He shrugs and pats me on the head, ruffling my hair. This isn't something he usually does. It feels awkward. I play along, batting at his hand until he stops, and then he walks to the front desk. I follow him. Once there he talks to the receptionist. He doesn't say specifically HIV or AIDS, but I'm not dumb. The receptionist hands him a clipboard of papers. He stands there and works on it until he's finished. When he gives it back, he asks how long it'll take for the results. The receptionist tells him that he'll have to talk to his doctor. Then we both go and sit and wait.

John's brought his Bible with him. He turns to a page in the middle. A verse is circled. It's God speaking to one of his followers. John reads it out loud to me, "Who then stands against me? Who has a claim that I must pay? Everything under heaven belongs to me."

I say, "What does that mean?"

"It means that, no matter what you do, how hard you try, how good a person you are, God may or may not give a shit in the end."

He closes the Bible and puts it onto the empty chair beside him. We sit and wait. I ask John if he remembers that Jordan play. I ask if he's ever seen anybody do that before. John starts telling me how Jordan is probably the best player in the NBA right now, but someday he'll be on the other side of a play like that. Then the receptionist calls his name.

Fridays are Friday Night Fellowship. John and I don't usually go when a game's on, but Cho says he's gonna put the game up on the projector, so we head over. Cho's got everyone in the cafeteria because he got the aunties to make food, and there's no food allowed in the sanctuary. The aunties are still there, standing by the chow mein and fried chicken with tongs. They hand me a plate. I thank them. They ask about our father. I say that he's doing great, even though I have no idea how he is. They look at me like they know the truth. I thank them again and find a seat in the front. John comes and sits next to me. He doesn't get any food, just a Coke from the machine.

At halftime, John says that we should head out. We'll watch the rest at home. I protest and then Cho gets up on the stage and says that they've put together a special halftime show. Music comes on. It's the song from Rocky, not "Eye of the Tiger," but the instrumental theme song. On the screen, there's a fade in and we see a bunch of guys in Laker and Bulls jerseys playing basketball. It's Cho and some other guys from church. I look for John, but John's not in it. Then there's a cool graphic that says: Poseur's Comp Returns!

The video is them reenacting highlights from Game Two. It's mostly terrible. The kids aren't even really trying to do the plays right. They're just goofing around. But the production looks really good. And there's music and also a play-by-play announcer who sounds just like Marv Albert. Then, as the final highlight, they have that Jordan hand-switching layup. It's Cho as Jordan and this tall kid named Benson Liu as Sam Perkins. Benson puts his hands up. He's supposed to try and block Cho, but he doesn't. He just stands there. Cho takes the pass and comes into the lane to dunk. He can't dunk in real life, but in the video they have the rim lowered. It doesn't matter because he switches hands just like Jordan did and lays it in on the other side. Then he does the fist pumping thing and that part looks exactly right.

When the video's over, I turn to John, but he's gone. He's over by the Coke machine again. He gets two drinks this time, one for me. When he gets back, I ask him if he saw Cho. He says that he saw it. I ask him if he liked it. He says, "Yeah, it was good."

Then the game starts up again. The Lakers go on a big run, and then the Bulls go on a big run. Then toward the very end, it goes back and forth. Bulls score, Lakers score, Lakers score again to make it a two-point Lakers lead. And then Jordan ties it all up, and the game goes to overtime.

This should be an exciting moment. I feel like the Lakers have a chance now. And if they win this game, then I'm pretty sure they'll win the series. I look over, and John seems like he's not paying attention. I say to him to pay attention to the game. He sort of snaps out of whatever he's thinking about, and says, "Oh shit, overtime." But almost as soon as we're both paying attention again, the Lakers start to struggle and then pretty soon after that, the game's over and they lose.

～

Game Four: Sunday, June 9. The Lakers come out strong, but their hopes are dashed when James Worthy is forced to leave the game due to injury. The Bulls dominate in the second half, closing out the contest on a 19–8 run. Final Score: Bulls 97– Lakers 82.

Cho's sermon is about this guy Job, God's number one most obedient guy in the Bible. Number one guy, that is, until one day, God and Satan make a bet to see how obedient Job will be if they kill all Job's kids, take away all his money, and make him sick. Cho is really into it. He puts a diagram up on the overhead. The diagram is impossible to make sense of. But the way Cho boils it down is that we all have just two choices to pick from: Jesus or Despair. And that no matter how bad things get, it's still those same two choices.

Cho says, "Job's wife tells him to choose despair. She says to him, Go on! Curse God and die! But Job knows he hadn't done anything wrong. He doesn't deserve all this evil. He has every right to curse God. But does he? Does he?"

I look at John. He has one arm draped over the back of the pew. I elbow him and whisper, "Cho's getting worked up." John doesn't say anything, but then he elbows me back and motions his head for the door. We both get up and head out. John doesn't look back, but I do. I see Cho. He sees me too. He doesn't wave, but he smiles a little and nods his head at me like he and I are still cool even though I'm leaving in the middle of his sermon.

One the way home, I ask John about the sermon, "Why would God agree to torture his best guy on a bet?"

Cho had said that God's reason for doing the bet isn't important. Cho had said God can do whatever he wants. Because we humans can't ever really understand God's reasons. And if we dare to ask? More often than not, God will just dunk on us. That's exactly how Cho said it, "God will dunk on your ass! Put you on a poster. 'Cause God is Jordan. And us? We're just Sam Perkins. Look it up! It's in the Bible."

I ask John if that's really in the Bible.

John says, "Jordan didn't dunk on Perkins. It was a layup."

Game Five: Wednesday, June 12. Without James Worthy, the Lakers lean heavily on Magic Johnson, who leads them to a slim fourth-quarter lead. But Chicago once again goes on a late run, squashing the Lakers' meager hopes and securing the championship. Michael Jordan will hoist his first of six NBA trophies. Meanwhile, Magic Johnson will abruptly retire before the start of the next season. Final Score: Bulls 108–Lakers 101.

When John gets off the phone, he's pretty quiet. He says for me to go read a book, he's going back down to CSUN. I tell him that I want to go with him. He tells me that he doesn't want me to go. He says, "There's no reason for you to come, Chris."

I say, "Is it bad?"

He takes a breath and nods a little bit.

He says, "Yeah, it's bad."

We don't know it yet, but that night's game will be the final game of the series. John and I watch together, and then Cho comes over with a pizza and a case of beer. The two of them drink and smoke cigarettes. Cho tells me to not ever say anything about the cigarettes at church. Then the two of them argue about the game. John keeps saying that it'd be different if Worthy wasn't injured. Cho keeps saying that no team has ever come back from down three to one. John keeps telling Cho to shut the fuck up with that negative energy. Cho says, "I don't make the rules son. I just play by them." Then Cho keeps calling John son. John tells him to quit that shit, and that Cho's a bandwagoning traitor because he's now suddenly a Bulls fan. Cho just responds to everything John says by calling him, son. "Whatever, son. Whatever, son." John says, "You're the son, bitch. You're the son." I join in too, saying, "What's up, son. What's up." And John and I team up against Cho, and we all three play wrestle, knocking over the beers, but laughing, and it all seems like old times.

Meanwhile, the game keeps slipping further away from us. My guy, AC Green, is being dominated by Jordan, who'll end up with 30 points. In the end, it's close on the scoreboard, but we never seem like we have a real chance. It all feels inevitable, like everyone knows it doesn't matter if we take the lead again, or if even we win this game, or even if we win the next one. We aren't the best team anymore. It's these other guys now, the new heroes, doing things like as if touched by the hand of God, directed by the hand of fate. It isn't anything we're doing wrong. It's just that, that which we are, we are.

At the end, the final score is Bulls 108–Lakers 101, and the series to the Bulls, 4 to 1. Chicago will go on to win six of the next eight NBA championships. Meanwhile, Los Angeles will struggle on and off the court in ways we cannot yet imagine.

But that night, in that game, there's this one break away with AC and Magic. One of our guys dislodges the basketball from Jordan's hands. AC takes the ball out of the air and drives down the sideline. Magic follows on the other wing. They pass it back and forth between them like it's rehearsed. Seamless, almost metered, like a ballet or a poem. For that play, everything is like it always was. AC ends up with the ball at the basket and casually dunks it with one hand. He stands for a second after scoring and looks into the crowd, into the TV camera too. The Forum crowd cheers and cheers. John and Cho cheer, high-fiving each other hard over and over. I cheer too. I cheer and do a little dance in front of the TV and pick up Cho's beer and take as big a swig as I can. Cho just laughs and says for me to go on and enjoy myself. And so, I do. So, we all do, and on the TV, AC just nods and half-smiles and walks back, getting ready for the next play.

IF I WERE THE OCEAN,
I'D CARRY YOU HOME

Paul drives west on the 10 Freeway, over the 405. His step-daughter is in the backseat. She is seven years old. Her name is Scharlene. She asks him where her father is. Paul doesn't want to tell her where her father is. He doesn't want to tell her where he actually is, but he also doesn't want to lie to her about where her father is either. He doesn't want to lie because he had promised her to always tell her the truth, a promise he made when her father, Tomas, first introduced them. Paul had knelt down and tried to shake her hand, but she wouldn't shake his hand. He had then said that he respected her reticence. He couldn't tell if she understood what he was saying. She had not looked like she understood. Then it had occurred to Paul to make a deal with her. If Scharlene would give him a chance, he promised to always to tell her the truth. She still would not shake Paul's hand, but she did smile and that seemed enough.

It's now two years into that promise. Paul has kept his end of their deal. It was easier than he expected, until today. To-day, he starts by trying to tell Scharlene what Tomas told him to tell her, that Tomas has to go away for work. This is not untrue, but it's also not really true either.

Paul then tries to tell Scharlene what is really true: Tomas left to go live in Chengdu, China. No, they are not going with him. Yes, Paul is Chinese, Chinese American. No, Paul has never been to Chengdu and actually had never heard of it before Tomas's news. As for Scharlene, Scharlene is now supposed to go live with Priscilla, Scharlene's mother, whom she hasn't seen since she was a baby.

Paul doesn't tell her any of that either.

Scharlene looks at him for what feels like a long time. Paul looks back at Scharlene. Then Scharlene looks out the window.

Paul exhales and goes back to trying to figure out where he's going.

He's heading toward Priscilla's apartment, or at least the last place that he remembers that Priscilla lived. He takes his cell phone and tries calling her. He's not sure if he has the right number. He hasn't talked to Priscilla in a long time. The phone rings. Nobody answers. It goes to voicemail. The voicemail is not Priscilla's voice. It's the robot voice. The robot voice recites the phone number. Paul hangs up.

He can't remember the name of Priscilla's street. He knows it was close to a small airport. He finds the airport. He circles the airport. Planes fly overhead. They look like old-timey planes. Small, noisy propeller planes. Then Paul passes Sendagaya Station, the bar they used to go to. When he sees Sendagaya Station, the directions come back to him. He turns a corner onto what he's pretty sure is Priscilla's street. Then about halfway down the block, he finds Priscilla's apartment building.

The shape of the building looks the same as Paul remembers. It's a two-story complex with ten units, maybe twelve. It looks the same except now there's a chain-link fence and the grass has been paved over. Priscilla was in apartment number one, on the first floor, up in front, facing the street. Its door is closed but the curtains are open. Paul can see someone through the window, a woman. It has to be her.

He puts the car in park but leaves the engine running. He checks on Scharlene. She's asleep. He takes another look at the building. He takes out his cell phone and redials Priscilla's number. This time someone answers.

"Pri? Is this Priscilla Zhou?"

"Who's this?"

Paul sighs. He knows the voice, low and always tired-sounding. And he can see her now, through the window talking on her cell phone. They talk for a minute, maybe two. They start with small talk, "How are you? Oh my God. It's been so long. It has. I've been okay. How's Tomas. Oh. How's the baby."

Then after the small talk, "Oh. China? Really? The baby's still here in LA. No. I don't know. I don't."

Then Priscilla says, "Wow."

Paul says, "Tomas wants you to take her."

"No?"

"That's what he said."

"Wow, Paulie. It's really a bad time though. I'm actually up north right now. On a job. Don't really know when I'll be back in LA."

Paul sighs. He watches Priscilla pace.

He says, "I'm outside your apartment. I can see you through your window."

"What?" she says. "That can't be. I'm in Fresno, man."

Paul gets out of the car, walks toward the building. He's still on his phone. The car is still running.

"What are you doing? This is your child we're talking about."

Priscilla doesn't respond. Paul keeps walking.

"Pri? Come on."

Paul gets to her door and knocks. There's no answer. He knocks again and shouts for Priscilla to answer. There's no answer. He tries the doorknob. It's locked. He stands at the door and waits for a second. He's still holding his cell phone to his ear. He then walks over to the window and looks in. There's not much to see, a big TV and a long couch. He doesn't see Priscilla. He looks back to the car and worries if Scharlene is okay. He waits for another few seconds. Every second feels very long. He then hangs up his phone and puts it back in his pocket and walks back to the car.

Paul pulls into the beach parking lot. He turns off the engine. Scharlene wakes up when he turns off the engine. She asks again about Tomas.

Paul says, "Your dad's not feeling well."

Scharlene looks at him. She doesn't look like she believes him.

Paul says, "Your dad's getting some rest right now."

Paul doesn't say anything more. He gets out of the car. He looks up. There's a glare from the sun. His eyes adjust. He looks at Scharlene. She's squinting. He puts a hat on her head. He looks at the hat. The hat's a little crooked. He adjusts the hat, pats her head, and then helps her out of the car.

The two of them walk toward the boardwalk. Scharlene seems tense. Her shoulders are hunched. She has her hands balled up into fists. Paul stops and kneels down. He takes one of her hands. She relaxes it. He puts his hand over hers. She grabs on. She looks worried. Then a man on a bicycle rides by with a loud radio strapped onto his handlebar. He comes close. Scharlene flinches.

Paul says, "You're okay."

Scharlene doesn't say anything back. Paul thinks maybe they should go home. He tells her again that she's okay. She still seems uncomfortable, but she starts walking.

Paul feels self-conscious as they make their way past a crowd in the parking lot. It's obvious to him that he and Scharlene are not related. Paul thinks he looks about as Chinese as humanly possible. He is short and fit, with a round face, narrow eyes, and thick, straight, perfectly black hair. He has always been self-conscious of his looks. Working out daily to bulk up and, until recently, dying his hair into a sandy blonde. Meanwhile, Scharlene has almost no trace of her mother's Asian ancestry. Instead, she's like a clone of Tomas. Her shoulders broad. Her arms and legs sinewy. She has a square jaw and rounded cheekbones, light hair and grey eyes. Paul imagines the crowd's suspicion, or at least curiosity. What's the deal with this Asian guy and this white little kid? But no one says anything.

The two of them reach the end of the parking lot. They go up the wooden steps to the boardwalk. Paul thinks of the boardwalk as a place for tourists. He calls it a capitalist carnival.

"Real LA people don't come here," he says.

"We're not real LA people?"

Paul laughs, and they both seem to loosen up a little bit.

They get up to the boardwalk. Scharlene looks around. There's a lot for her to see.

He says, "Go ahead. Whatever you want."

Scharlene looks up at Paul with a questioning look on her face. Paul isn't usually this relaxed about his money.

"Yes, I mean it."

She doesn't go, but she leans forward a little. Paul lets go of her hand and gives her a soft push. She doesn't budge. He takes her hand again.

"Okay. We'll do this together."

The two of them go. First, they play carnival games. They don't win anything. Paul jokes that the games are rigged. Scharlene doesn't seem to understand what he means.

Next, they ride carnival rides. The rides are shaky. Surprisingly, Scharlene isn't scared on the rides. This reminds him of Tomas, brave when it comes to physical things.

Next, Paul buys her a conch shell. Scharlene holds it to his ear. He doesn't hear anything.

He says, "I don't hear anything."

Scharlene laughs. Paul then buys her a blue parasol. It gets blown away by a gust of wind. He offers to buy another one, but Scharlene says, "No thank you." Then Paul buys her a framed Polaroid picture of Scharlene next to a cardboard cutout of the mighty Thor, because they both agree it looks like Tomas.

Slowly, they work their way to the quiet end of the board-walk. Scharlene stops at a woman sitting on a heavy blanket. The blanket has wooden toys on it. Scharlene looks at each toy. Some are animals. Some are people. Some are things like cars or treasure chests. Scharlene picks up a boat.

She says, "I like this one."

The woman says, "It's gopher wood."

Paul says, "Like Noah's Ark?"

Paul laughs and then reaches out and takes the boat from Scharlene.

He says, "Maybe I'll keep this one for my office."

Scharlene snatches the boat back from Paul's hand.

Paul shouts at her before he can stop himself.

"No!"

Scharlene is startled. She looks down. Her eyes get teary. She holds the boat out to Paul.

Paul exhales and rubs his face. He looks at Scharlene. She looks scared but also angry. He puts both hands on the boat. He tries to push the boat back to her. He tries not to push too hard. Scharlene resists by locking her elbows. The pointy end of the boat digs into the palm of Paul's hand. He pushes the boat a little bit hard, but Scharlene still won't take it back. Paul stops pushing.

He looks at her and wants to say that this is all unfair. That he's not the bad guy here. He's the good guy. He wants to grab hold of Scharlene and tell her that he is the good guy here. He wants to make her see that. That this is not his fault. That this is neither his fault nor his responsibility. But all really just an act of goodness on his part. And isn't he hurt here as well?

Doesn't he deserve some care and sympathy? Someone to buy him candy and toys?

He can feel his eyes tear up now. He wants to break the boat. He squeezes the boat very hard, but it doesn't break.

Then he exhales, and then he breathes in.

He exhales again.

He relaxes his hold on the boat.

He says, "Good, quick reflexes. Like a cat."

Paul does not like cats, but he knows Scharlene likes cats. When he talks about cats, he thinks of it as some kind of code to let her know that the two of them are on the same team. He doesn't know if she understands.

Paul gives the boat back to Scharlene. She holds it for a second and then puts it back down on the woman's blanket. Paul exhales again, but now not so much in a frustrated way as in a tired way. He thinks about how sensitive Scharlene and Tomas are. How can such physically strong people be so emotionally fragile?

Paul takes out his billfold.

"How much for the boat."

The woman frowns.

"Six dollars."

Paul gives her a ten and says to keep the change. The woman takes the money without thanking him. He picks up the boat with one hand and reaches out his other hand to Scharlene. She takes his hand. They walk back down the boardwalk. They don't talk for a little while. Then, Scharlene starts talking about the rides and then the candy and then the umbrella. Paul nods his head. He's still a little mad, but he's also happy that things seem back to normal.

By the time they get to where the tarmac meets the sand, Scharlene looks tired. Paul puts her things into his backpack. He takes out a pack of cigarettes and shakes it. There's one cigarette left. He takes it out and then puts it back. Then he puts the backpack back on. Then he picks Scharlene up and puts her up on his shoulders.

Paul looks out across the beach as he walks. He's surprised at how big everything looks. The sand seems to go on forever like a desert from out of the Bible. And the sky too. It stretches out like a big blue tarp. Then, he thinks, the ocean is like God, mumbling in a secret language. He listens as he walks. He feels the sand spray behind him. Scharlene is still on his shoulders. When they get close to the water, Paul finds a dry spot. He rolls up his pants legs. He opens the backpack and takes out a clipboard. He starts to dig out a flat spot. He calls it, "the base."

He then starts piling wet sand on to the base. He forms it into a stack of blocks. Scharlene seems to realize what he's doing.

Scharlene says, "Sandcastle?"

Paul stands up.

"Correct. And you are in charge of hydro-engineering."

Scharlene looks at him.

"Get the water."

Scharlene nods.

Paul says, "This is not a child's job. This is real work. Are you sure you can handle it?"

Scharlene salutes him.

"Yes, sir."

Paul laughs.

He salutes back.

He hands her the bucket. Scharlene wades into the surf, splashing her feet as she goes. She gets about waist high and starts to fill the bucket. Then a wave comes and knocks her off balance. The water spills. She fills the bucket again. The same thing happens. She looks up at Paul. He can tell she is frustrated. He thinks it'd be easier to get the water for her, but instead he pretends not to see her, making a show of carving out the notches on the castle walls. Scharlene frowns and halfheartedly scoops at the water. The bucket fills halfway and then gets dumped out and then gets filled halfway again. Then a wave comes in. Scharlene holds the half-full bucket, and it doesn't spill. Her eyes widen. She looks up to Paul. She wraps her arms around the bucket. She lugs it up through the surf, up the shore, and back to the castle. When she gets to Paul, he takes the bucket and pours it out around the castle.

Paul says, "We'll need more."

He looks at her from the corner of his eye. She claps her hands together and hurries back to the water. Paul goes back to work. Scharlene gets more water. Paul keeps acting like he's too busy with his own work to notice how happy she is. Scharlene doesn't seem to mind the lack of attention. This goes on for a while. Then, before he knows it, Paul is almost done. He's just finishing the tower. The tower is tricky because it's so tall and also skinny. Paul takes his time. He just has one more thing to do, a little window on the top floor.

"That will be your room, Charley."

Scharlene nods.

"What about your room?"

Paul thinks. He thinks he needs a big room for his many books. He also thinks he'd like nice lighting, and also a view of the ocean. Keeping all that in mind, he points to the south-west corner of the castle.

"That will be my office. So I can watch the sunset."

"That's a good one."

She looks up at Paul.

"And Daddy?"

"Your dad?" says Paul. "Well, what about your mom?"

Scharlene looks at Paul like she doesn't know what he's talking about.

"Your mom might want a room in the castle."

"No, you know my mom doesn't live with us."

"Oh," he says. "Okay."

"What about Daddy though?"

"Daddy? Well, as for your dad. Let me see."

Paul looks around the castle. He tries to picture Tomas in the tower with Scharlene or in the office with him, but both of those feel wrong. He tries to picture Tomas in the courtyard, practicing sword fighting or bow and arrow or just having a laugh with the other knights. Tomas would like that, but it's still not quite right. Then Paul reaches into his backpack and takes out the toy boat. He holds it up in front of Scharlene. He points at the little steering wheel and captain's chair.

"Here," he says. "Here is where Tomas will live."

Scharlene takes the boat and holds it up to her face, right up to the tip of her nose.

"Here?" she says.

The two of them look at the boat. They look over the deck

from front to back and to the front again. They focus in on the little captain's chair.

"Yes," says Paul. "Here, right here."

Scharlene takes the boat to the castle. Scharlene looks over the sandcastle. She checks the top of the tower from a few different angles. Then she puts the toy boat on the top of it. She moves it around a little to make sure it's level. When she's done, she lays down on her stomach and rests her cheek on a warm pillow of dry sand. Paul leans himself back onto his elbows. He takes out his last cigarette. He twirls it in his fingers. He imagines this tiny sandcastle version of his family. Scharlene is the princess. Tomas is the king. Paul is also a king. Then he thinks that it's odd to have the one king stuck in a boat. It's like a kind of a jail, but a safe and loving jail.

The tide quietly rises as Paul thinks about Tomas in the boat. It creeps up the shore a little bit at a time, a little bit and a little bit. The sun starts leaning toward the horizon. Clouds float through the sky and pass in front of the sun. The sunbeams poke through the gaps. One beam shines onto Scharlene like it's directed by some angelic stagehand.

The first wave to reach the castle just touches and then retreats. The next wave does the same. This goes on until a small corner of sand gives way and collapses. Paul sees this and looks to Scharlene. She gets up off the sand and goes around to the broken corner. She looks worried. Then, another wave comes and takes another chunk out of the same corner. Scharlene jumps back. She runs over to Paul.

Scharlene says, "The castle is breaking."

She says more, a frantic tone in her voice. It is hard to understand all of what she's saying. She is already so upset, and Paul can feel himself getting upset because Scharlene is upset. He feels like he has to fix this for her. Then he's mad that he can't. Then he realizes he's really waited too long to tell her about Tomas.

Paul says, "Scharlene, sit with me for a minute."

She points to the castle.

Paul says, "I need to tell you something. Something important."

She pulls his arm. She doesn't seem interested in what Paul has to say. But Paul doesn't budge. So, Scharlene sits.

Paul says, "The world of adults is much more complicated than the world of children."

Scharlene says, "I know that."

"Yes," he says. "You know that, but there are things you know here."

He taps her forehead.

"But that you don't yet know here."

He taps her sternum.

Scharlene says, "The heart."

"Yes. So, you understand what I'm talking about? You can know something like from a book or from a story, but it's not the same until it happens to you."

Scharlene squints at him. Paul points to the toy boat.

"It's like Noah. We teach that story to children your age. You understand what happened. He collected the animals, the flood came, and he sailed in his boat until the flood was over. It's a nice story. Right?"

"There weren't any sails on Noah's ark."

Despite himself, this makes Paul laugh.

"So," he continues. "For us it's a fun story. But think about it for Noah. For Noah, it wasn't fun. It was really scary. God tells him to do this very strange and scary thing. And he does it, but then he has to see everyone he's ever known drown in the ocean. Gone. Everything. People he knew since he was little. His friends. His neighbors. His family. His mommy, and then his daddy."

Scharlene nods.

"Yes, yes, I understand."

But she's only a kid. Paul doesn't think she really understands.

He says, "The ocean will take everything, eventually."

Scharlene looks at him with a confused look on her face.

"Not everything. The ocean didn't take Noah."

"Well, I guess not."

"And the ocean didn't take Noah's animals."

"No, I guess not them either."

This is not the point that Paul wants to make. He wants to explain something about loss to Scharlene, but he's not saying it right. He tries to think of a better way to say it, but nothing comes to mind. Meanwhile, Scharlene looks impatient.

Paul gets up. He puts his still-unlit last cigarette in his mouth.

"Okay, then," he says. "Let's get started."

They walk up the shore toward a pile of driftwood. Paul tells Scharlene they need the wood for a wall. She runs off to get the wood. Paul watches the waves come in. A small wave hits the castle and brings down what was supposed to be Paul's office. Scharlene drops an armful of branches and runs toward the castle. Paul follows after her.

They work out a little system. Paul piles the branches while Scharlene sods the pile with wet sand. This holds for a while. The wall redirects the smaller waves and absorbs the bigger ones. But each wave breaks down a little bit of the wall. The sand melts and the wood gets washed away. The two keep working, but the tide keeps coming in deeper. Paul finds a long, paddle shaped branch. He uses the paddle to dig a trench about a foot in front of the castle. He calls it the moat. Scharlene does the same with the clipboard. Then she gives up on the clipboard and starts using her arms and legs to block the water, laying down as a human barricade.

This goes on for a while, but it is, as Paul knew from the start, a lost cause. Eventually, the tide comes in too far and overtakes the moat, then the wall, and then finally the castle itself. By this time, Scharlene can barely lift her arms to shoo away the water. She lays limp like a washed-up ocean animal. Paul picks her up and carries her the four or five feet to dry land. She lifts her head up to look at Paul. He holds her by the armpits and looks into her eyes. She pats him on the top of his head.

Scharlene says, "Good job, Daddy."

Paul looks at her. He tilts his head to the side and wonders if she called him that on purpose, but it doesn't seem like it.

Paul says, "Good job to you."

Scharlene says, "We'll make another one tomorrow."

And Paul says, "Of course."

She pulls away and goes back to the water, about knee-high. She's wobbly, but looks okay. He follows her. Together they step around, feeling with their feet for their castle, but it is just flat smooth sand now.

As they feel around the ocean floor with their toes, Paul sees the toy boat float by. It sways with the tide, rushing toward the beach. Then it's still for a second before being carried back out. Paul tries to wade over to it. At about chest high, Paul closes in, but a receding pull carries the boat past his reach. He thinks he might be able to get to it if he swims. He might, he thinks, as he watches the boat being carried further and further away, until it's lost in the swells and shadows.

And then he hears a voice through the noisy surf and wind. The voice says, "Paul!"

Paul turns back to the shoreline. He sees Scharlene waving at him. What's left of the sunlight shines on her. The noise from the ocean rumbles around him. It sounds a little bit like a song. Paul listens. Waves and waves and waves and then birds, some birds squawk as they fly overhead. Scharlene waves and waves. Paul waves back and starts to walk toward her.

"Charley," he says. "Are you okay?"

He wipes water from her face and tucks her hair behind her ears.

She says, "I'm okay."

"I was, I don't know. I was getting the boat. But I couldn't reach it."

"It's okay. I'm okay."

Paul picks her up and bounces her in the crook of his elbow to secure her balance. She wraps her arms around his neck and hugs him. He hugs her back. Then he starts walking to shore. They sway with the tide. When they get to the beach, they pass his backpack. Paul reaches down and picks it up with his free hand. He does this without slowing down. With the bag on one shoulder and Scharlene on his hip, everything feels balanced and light. Scharlene feels light. So light it's as if he can toss her up into the air, and she'd float away. But he doesn't toss her up into the air. He holds on to her. She leans her head on his shoulder. She's quiet for a second, and then startles as if she fell asleep and then suddenly woke up.

"I've got you," he says. "I've got you."

Scharlene nods and drops her head back onto his shoulder. As they make their way, she tells him what her favorite things about the beach are, and Paul picks the grains of sand out of her hair.

THE FATTED CALF

I'd forgotten how much darker it is on this side of the river, the night sky blocked out by the pines behind the houses. I lose my footing and drop to one knee on the wet clay between my dad's old place and our neighbor, Big Jay. I get steady by keeping one hand on Big Jay's fishing boat as I walk. I trace over the boat's registration numbers: VA-666-AF. We had always gotten a kick out of that. I laugh to myself about my supposed summer as Big Jay's junior boatman. I was so bad at it. Big Jay pulling the crab traps in, and me trying to sort. I'd just finished high school. Big Jay had offered me forty dollars a day. I convinced him to give me a two-week advance, which I never earned, having left town after my third day out.

On his porch, I lean my head on the screen-door. I can see the TV on, Fox News probably. In the kitchen, Big Jay is getting the coffee going, same as he always did, looking like a laboratory scientist, leveling out each scoop of grounds with a pinky finger before turning on the percolator. It isn't any kind of gourmet stuff, just store-bought and an old Coffee-mate machine. But I feel a homesickness for it all the same. Something about the way he moves, this big, thoughtful beast.

I take my satchel from under my arm and softly tap it against the handrail. There's four hundred dollars inside, just about how much I took for the crabbing that I hadn't done. I tuck the satchel into the back of my pants, and then knock. Big Jay does not seem at all alarmed to hear knocking at his door at three in the morning. He just says, "Hold up," as he finishes putting the grounds back into the fridge. When he gets to the door, almost before he could possibly have seen who it is, he says, "Well, if it isn't Princeton Moss."

I don't respond right away. The two of us stand at the open door for a second, looking each other over. Big Jay this large, white, middle-aged man, and me, this skinny Asian kid. Then, he says, "Been a while," and the two of us hug a hearty and hardy hug. When we're done, he holds me by the shoulders and looks me over again, "Look at you. I was just talking to Wilkes and them about how that Korean guy in Walking Dead's the spitting image of little Princeton. And here you are."

"Here I am."

"Well, shit. Here you are."

"Yes, sir."

"Now that I'm looking at you, you don't look anything like that guy."

"I don't know," I say. "I hear it all the time. You all aren't the first."

Big Jay just nods and then, as if he's suddenly regained all sense of himself, says, "Well, shit. Don't just stand there. Come on in."

"I know you're about to head out," I say. "I don't want to hold you up."

"It's no trouble," he says. "I haven't even had my coffee yet. And I'm guessing, you neither."

I drag my feet against the doormat, trying to scrape the mud. Big Jay says, "Don't worry about that. The place is a mess." But it's not a mess at all, so I kick off my shoes before I come in.

Big Jay pats me on the shoulder and directs me to the kitchen table. I take a chair, pulling the satchel out from my pants and laying it on my lap, not hiding it, but not making it obvious either. At the cupboard, Big Jay gets a second mug and pulls the half-brewed pot from the percolator, pouring a cup for me and one for himself, before putting the pot back on to finish.

"You still take cream, no sugar?"

"Black'll be fine."

"Well, all right then."

He sets the coffees down and picks up the remote and turns the TV off. Then he just sits and looks at me again, shaking his head as if he cannot believe his eyes.

I say, "You're creeping me out, man."

"Come on. Give an old man a break. I haven't seen you since, God, how long?"

"It's just been the two years. Not any time at all."

"Still, seems long to me."

"Yeah," I admit. "I guess same here."

Big Jay nods his head toward the kitchen and says, "You hungry? I can make some breakfast real quick. It'd be no trouble."

"No thank you, sir. I'm fine with coffee."

The two of us proceed to catch up a little bit. I ask Big

Jay how the crabbing's been. He says it's been good, really good actually. He's even thinking of getting a new boat, a bigger one. That little dinghy'd almost capsized twice this last season, one time seven bushels went over. Seven! He'd been so mad over that, for days he couldn't stop talking about it, to the point that the guys at the pool hall made him start buying a round every time he brought it up. But things were good. Lots of jimmies. I chuckle at that, the jimmies part. "Jimmies" are what boatmen call the ones you keep; the big, hard, grade-A, male blue crab.

"I always wondered," I say. "Is that why they call you Big Jay?"

"Why who calls me Big Jay?"

"Why people call you Big Jay, because of the crabs. The jimmies."

"You mean as in I catch the most jimmies or I'm the king of the jimmies or some such?"

Big Jay shrugs and so I shrug too. I'd never asked before, but I'd always assumed, not just because Big Jay is big, which he is, but also because he's a good one, grade-A, the kind that you want to keep.

"You're a good one, Big Jay."

"Now, what are you talking about?"

"Nothing. Just thinking about crabbing and jimmies and whatnot."

"Oh, Jesus," says Big Jay, shaking his head and heaving an exaggerated exhale. "Speaking of. You wouldn't believe what I'd pulled out of the bay."

I laugh, "I don't care to hear any fishing stories."

"Shit, you've never heard one like this."

Then Big Jay looks like he's hesitating, like he's maybe changed his mind about telling the story after all.

"Come on," I say. "What, is this not an ordinary fishing story? This is something particularly unusual? I want to hear it."

Big Jay says, "I shouldn't have mentioned it."

"Why?"

"It's disturbing."

"Oh shit," I say. "Was it a body? Oh my God, you found a body."

He waves both hands across his face.

"I'm telling you," says Big Jay. "It'll ruin you for crab."

"What?" I say.

"It'll ruin your appetite for crab."

I lean back, thinking about how blue crab, like all crab, will eat literally anything: plant, animal, living, dead. They eat shit even. They're even known to cannibalistically eat their own. But still, a human corpse, I'd never heard of that before.

I shake my head and say, "Oh, jeez."

Big Jay just says, "Yup."

I say, "Must've been pretty rotted out."

He again says, "Yup."

"Where were they at?"

"The crabs? Face, mostly. Some other spots."

"Oh, Jesus."

I point down to my crotch. Big Jay nods. Then he waves his hand in a big circle from his head down to his knees and back up again.

"All over."

"Dang," I say. "What do you do in that situation?"

"I was in the middle of my day. I still had a couple lines to run."

"Oh no. You didn't just, like, leave the body on your deck, did you?"

"No, no," says Big Jay. "Come on. What kind of person you think I am?"

I shrug. "You never know. I mean, there wasn't any helping him from that point on."

"Her," says Big Jay. "It was a girl."

"Oh."

"She was just a kid. I mean, though I couldn't tell exactly how old. Even the cops said it'd take the coroner to really know."

"Jesus."

"Yeah."

"It reminds me of that story."

"That what now?"

"Nothing," I say. "Just this old story about these guys on a fishing trip. They find a body of a girl floating in the river. They don't want to quit early on their trip though, so they anchor her to a tree so she won't float away. That way they can finish their fishing trip and then tell the cops about it when they're done. You know what I mean? After they're done with all the fishing and whatnot."

Big Jay shakes his head. "What kind of story is that?"

I say, "It's famous, man."

"I've never heard of it."

"There's that movie of it. It's got Huey Lewis as the guy who finds the body."

"Well, anyway. That's not realistic. Believe me. If you found a dead girl floating in the water, you wouldn't be able to go on fishing. No way."

"You think?"

"Yes. Yes, I do."

The two of us sip our coffees and settle back into our chairs. I stop talking about the dead girl. Big Jay doesn't say anything more either, and that seems like maybe what the guys in the story did, just stopped talking about it, even though they might not have been able to stop thinking about it. They might've just silently agreed to pretend that the body wasn't there, all of them colluding in the abdication.

Big Jay lets out a sigh like to indicate that that's enough about that, and he goes on and asks how I'm doing, how's Janet, how's everything. I tell him that we've been all right. The two of us, we're still together. I don't tell him that we're struggling a little with money. I also don't say anything yet about moving to California. Then Big Jay mentions that he'd seen Janet playing guitar with her dad's band, Funkyard Dog, over at The Mag. I laugh and ask what the fuck Big Jay's doing at The Mag, which is not a trendy people's place, but still too trendy for Big Jay. Big Jay puffs up his chest and says how he's not too old to cut a rug. I laugh at the cut-a-rug part.

Big Jay says, "Even an old boatman's gotta get loose now and again."

He does a little dance move with his shoulders. I say that's enough of that. And then I ask him what he thought of the band. He makes a fuss about how come I don't know myself how good my girl's band is. Some boyfriend!

I say, "It's her dad's band, not Janet's."

Big Jay says, "Anyway, they were great. Great."

"Janet doesn't even like funk music. She's just playing as a favor."

"Well, all the better. That's her father. He's her people. Isn't helping him a good enough reason? Even if she hates it, isn't family a good enough reason to go ahead and do it anyway, if you're able?"

Big Jay says this like he's trying to make a larger point.

I don't want to argue, but still, I say, "That's naïve, man. Her dad's taking advantage of her. He knows she's not into it. He's using her."

I shift in my chair. The satchel slips a little off my lap. I catch it before it falls and then prop it in-between my knees. Big Jay doesn't seem to notice. He shakes his head and then says something about how Janet's really good on the guitar, and then changes the subject all together and starts asking me about school. I realize that he doesn't know I graduated.

"Oh shit," I say. "I graduated, Big Jay. I'm done."

"Oh shit," he says. "Well, damn it, Princeton. Congratulations. Wow, you're a college graduate. My God. Congratulations."

I try to apologize for not telling him sooner. I say it's just junior college. He says he'd have liked to come to the ceremony. I tell him that there wasn't even a ceremony, even though there was. Then he asks what I'm doing now. I don't want to get into my leaving town, so I just say that I'm going to work on my book.

"That's good," he says. "That one about the spaceman?"

"Astronaut. But yeah, that one."

"That's good. I always liked that story. Reminded me of a *Twilight Zone* and whatnot."

This is true. I got the idea from a *Twilight Zone*, the one where astronauts land on a planet where everyone is frozen like statues. It turns out the planet is actually some kind of heaven, where everyone spends eternity in their favorite memory, whatever that memory is: the day they won a beauty pageant, the day they became mayor, the day they fished their limit, or what have you. The only catch is, they're all still dead and the whole scene is frozen like some kind of diorama, like a taxidermy display, like one of those caveman scenes at a human history museum.

"You gonna make a movie of it?"

"No, man. They wouldn't make a movie of it."

"Well, I'm sure you could."

"I don't think so," I say. "I'm not gonna show up in Hollywood and try to sell them an old *Twilight Zone*, even if it is all rewritten."

"Hollywood?"

"Yeah."

"You're going to Hollywood."

"Yeah."

Big Jay frowns a little. He takes a sip of his coffee. I do too. It's cold. He gestures to the coffeemaker, and I push my cup over to him. He gets up and warms up both. He takes a sip of the warmed-up coffee as he's sitting back down.

"That's better."

I sip mine too.

Big Jay says, "So, Hollywood. When you taking off?"

"Tomorrow," I say. "Janet made the decision, so I'm going too."

This isn't completely true. It is true she mentioned it first.

But I'm the one who applied to schools out there. I'm the one who found a place to live. It's as much me as her.

I say, "You know Virginia's never been particularly good to me, present company excluded, of course."

"Yeah, sure," he says, and then, "I mean, I do understand. I know you never really took to this life."

He waves a hand around.

"No, I haven't."

"Well, LA will be like a homecoming." He says, referring to how I was born in California, a ways outside of Los Angeles, but we'd always just said I was from LA.

"Yeah, sort of," I say. "You know, I've lived here now twice as long as I'd lived there."

Big Jay says, "Hmm, true."

"Virginia always stayed kinda foreign to me. Or I guess, I'm the foreign one, like a visitor, like the astronaut from my story. Like I landed on this alien planet and it looks like home, but it's not." I look at Big Jay to make sure I haven't offended him. I can't tell. I go on, "It just never quite felt right. I don't know. It's stupid things like the warm ocean water, the winter snow, thunderstorms, all those trees, the Confederate stuff, even if it's supposed to be just heritage and decoration, which I guess it mostly is."

"It doesn't suit everyone."

"Yeah, no, I guess not."

"Well, but, Hollywood," Big Jay says, "I can see that, for you both. Show business."

I say, "Yeah, sure. Yeah, sure."

Then I try to explain why I'm here, even though Big Jay isn't asking. I apologize for coming so late and unannounced.

I tell him how I'd been out late, a kind of a goodbye party. Then I apologize for not inviting him to the party. Then I apologize again for coming over so late.

"I don't know what's wrong with me."

"You're always welcome here, kid. I ain't got nowhere to be."

"Yeah," I say. "We'd just been out late. I couldn't sleep so I was just driving around. I just thought I'd stop by since it's been a while."

Big Jay listens, letting me keep talking about where else I'd been that night, until he says, "You need cash?"

"No, no," I say. "No, sir. I do not."

"For your trip?"

"No, sir," I say, and then, "It's the opposite, Big Jay. I want to pay you back, for that money I took for the crabbing I didn't do."

He says, "Shit, kid. I don't need your money."

"It's your money. It was a loan. I'm just here to pay it back."

I finish the coffee in my mug. Big Jay then gets up and goes over to his secretary desk. He pulls down the trap and takes out a billfold. He counts out six hundred dollars, all in hundred-dollar bills, and brings it over.

He says, "This is for you and Janet. Consider it an advance on your wedding gift."

I push the money back to him and say, "What're you doing?"

I take out the satchel. I tell him I'm the one here to give him money. I take out the four hundred, a stack of twenties. I put it on the table and push it toward him, so that all the money now is in one pile. Big Jay looks away and makes a show like he's pretending like he's trying not to laugh.

"I appreciate you," he says. "But you don't need to worry

about this. I never expected this money back. And where I'm going, I'm not gonna need it."

"What do you mean, where you're going?"

"It's nothing," he says. "Forget I said that."

"Where are you going, Big Jay?"

Big Jay doesn't answer. I ask again, and he just keeps shrugging as if he'd misspoke. I get up from my chair. I pick up both coffee mugs, now both empty, and go over to the coffeemaker.

Big Jay says, "It's all drank, but you know where it's at if I want to brew another pot."

I go ahead and start another pot going. As I'm doing this, Big Jay stays seated, carefully putting the money on the table into one pile, the hundreds on the bottom and the twenties on top.

He says, "Princeton?"

I say, "Where are you going, Big Jay?"

"That debt really all you're here for?"

"I'm serious," I say. "What do you mean by, you're not gonna need that money where you're going?"

Big Jay folds his arms and says, "I'm selling the house. Wilkes been wanting to expand the compound, and I don't need all this land anyway. I can live on the boat or just rent a place. It's not a big deal. It's not."

"Fucking Wilkes," I say.

"Wilkes's not doing anything wrong."

As Big Jay says this, he doesn't look at me. I don't know why, except maybe that he's embarrassed. Then he goes on and says how he's thinking of getting a regular job. The post office is hiring. It's not the great job it used to be, no benefits anymore really, but it's a steady paycheck. As he's still going on about it, I put a hand on his shoulder and say, "I'm sorry."

"Hey, I said I'm fine, kid. I'm good, okay?"

"Okay."

"Okay."

We nod in a kind of unison, then he says, "Shoot. I swear to God, I thought you were gonna say something like you'd gotten Janet pregnant or something."

I say, "Shit, I thought you were gonna say you had cancer or something."

We chuckle over that a little bit. I shake my head and then look over at the money on the table. One thousand dollars. I know I need it, but despite what he said, I know Big Jay needs it too. I should leave it. I know I should do that. I should leave the money. It's really his anyway, his six and then the four that I'd owed him. It's really his money, all of it.

Big Jay says, "Hold up. I got something else. I almost forgot."

He goes into his hall closet. He comes back not more than a minute later with a cardboard box. The shape and size of it is nothing special, but still, I know it right away. It's my old toy box from when I was a kid. It'd gone missing years ago, tucked away and then lost. But I'd thought about it every once in a while. I'd wondered if it'd been thrown out or sold or, less likely, given away to some other kid.

Big Jay says, "Wilkes brought this over when they were doing the demo on your old house. I'd told him I'd hold on to it, in case you ever came around. And now, here you are. So, here it is."

Big Jay puts the box on the table. I get up and open the box flaps. Most of it is stuff I forgot about, some GI Joes, Matchbox cars, a baseball, a sock full of marbles. But then there's the one thing I'd been missing, my favorite thing from when I was a kid: a model of the Space Shuttle with an action figure of a NASA astronaut.

"Holy moly, Big Jay."

"Yeah. I remember you toting that around everywhere. You took it out on my boat once when you were little, remember that?"

"I do remember that."

"You leaning over the stern with that shuttle up into the wind."

I can picture it as he says this. I can feel it, the cold morning air biting at my eyeballs, and that toy feeling like it was lifting off into outer space.

"That was a good day."

"The best."

I take a breath and say thank you. Big Jay looks like he's going to say, it's nothing. Before he does, I say, "I don't know if I ever told you, but you were really good to me when no one else was."

"Yeah," says Big Jay, without really pausing much. "Well, you deserved better."

The two of us then stand over the toys, not speaking for another good couple seconds, wanting this moment to hurry and be over with, but also hanging on to it too. Then I put my hand out to shake. Big Jay goes ahead and takes my hand, and the two of us shake. When that's done, he says, "I'm gonna get going."

I say, "Shit, sorry, Big Jay."

"You need to go home and get some rest."

"Yeah."

"Yeah."

I pick up the box and turn toward the front door. I don't take the money.

I say. "You have a good one."

Big Jay says, "Yeah, you too."

At the door, I get my shoes on and think about postponing the trip, staying in town a little longer. I turn around and tell Big Jay, "We should all get together. We'll do a crab boil. Go all out, oysters and clams too. Get Wilkes to smoke some big piece of meat. We can get the whole block, everybody together like old times. We'll do that."

Big Jay laughs and says, "Sounds good."

He puts my satchel in the box. It's zipped up, but I already know all one thousand is in it. I think to make a fuss, try to give it back to him, make a show of it. But I already know I'm going to take it, so all that show would be more disrespectful than anything. So, I don't say anything more. I just nod and turn and then walk the short bit to Janet's car, that old box under one arm as I go.

Part Two

MAIN & MAINE

They know of each other in the coincidental kind of way. She is the cousin of his cousin's boyfriend. Also, they have almost the same last name. His is Chiang. Hers is Chang. All this makes it sound like they are related, but they aren't. When they first meet in real life, he sees her in the kitchen at a party. She's drinking a soda out of the can. She's got something baking in the oven, like a dessert. She takes it out. It's graham crackers and some kind of yellow sauce. It looks terrible, but she looks great, pretty like in her pictures, but pale and also shorter. Less Korean, if that makes sense, less assertive, less sociable. He guesses those kinds of things show differently in pictures.

But she moves like she's floating in water, out of time with the music, but in time with the deep, the invisible, like she's one with God or the ocean. These are the kinds of things he might say to describe someone he wants to sleep with. He does want to sleep with her. He also thinks he could be in love with her, but she isn't available and neither is he. So, he keeps his distance. He hides out in the kitchen. He drinks several beers. He keeps count in his head. Seven. That's too many. He's drunk, maybe. He's a quiet drunk. He is also a quiet sober person.

She keeps coming to talk to him as if they're flirting. He doesn't think she is good at flirting. He is not good at flirting. He doesn't know for sure that they're flirting, but she touches his arm when she talks to him. This is maybe the fourth time she's touched his arm like this. She says, "I don't know why I keep touching your arm."

He pays close attention to her exact words: "I don't know why I keep touching your arm." He tries to interpret this. He wants it to tell him that she wants to sleep with him. He also wants it to tell him how to talk to her. He wants to say things to her. He can feel his heart in his throat.

Then the moment passes.

Her boyfriend comes and joins their conversation. Her boyfriend's name is Walt Gourley. Walt is a tall, muscular Scots-Irish guy with Pokémon tattoos up and down his left arm. He likes Walt. He's a fan of Pokémon. And also, Walt talks a lot, which means he doesn't have to talk as much.

Walt says, "Who's this?"

He wonders why Walt doesn't recognize him. They go to the same school. They're almost the same major. His is Literature. Walt's is Creative Writing.

She says, "This is James Chiang's cousin."

He puts his hand out to Walt. He's about to introduce himself when Walt slaps his hand away and gives him a hug. "Hey, no way, Jimmy Chiang's cousin? I fucking love Jimmy."

Walt holds him for a long time. It's a full contact hug, chest to chest, stomach to stomach, penis to penis. He arches his back to keep their penises from touching. It doesn't help.

Walt is very strong. He gives in. He relaxes. He hugs Walt back. It feels really great. He is about to lay his head on Walt's shoulder when Walt lets go, keeping one arm around his neck, Walt grabs her with the other arm so it's a Walt sandwich, him to the left and her to the right. He wonders if something sexual could happen with the three of them. It's not exactly what he wants, but he wouldn't say no either.

Then his girlfriend calls from across the room. He sees her calling. She's hard to miss. She is tall and has bright blonde hair. It's amazing, and it's her real hair.

Walt says, "That your girl?"

He nods, "Maggie."

He waits for Walt to say something approving. Walt doesn't say anything approving. Maggie motions for him to come over. Walt holds tight and then motions for Maggie to come to them. Maggie tilts her head to the side and frowns.

He says, "I better go."

Walt grabs the back of his neck and shakes him gently, and says, "Alright, Jimmy's cousin. Take it easy then."

He looks past Walt and says, "See you later, Hanna."

It's loud. He doesn't know if Hanna hears him. He turns and starts to walk to Maggie. As he gets turned around, he feels a slap on his ass. He turns back. It's Walt.

Maggie takes the beer from his hand. It's still cold. She takes a sip. She asks him who invited those two, meaning Hanna and Walt. He doesn't say anything. He just shrugs. It's his most common gesture.

He doesn't want to be with Maggie. He keeps trying to think of ways to break up with her. He's not sure why he doesn't want to be with her, except maybe it's because she's too tall for him. She's taller than him by almost an inch. Also, her hair is itchy. And also, he doesn't know if she likes him. She's never said anything, but he thinks she also wants to break up, and she's trying to make him do it. But he's trying to make her do it. He admits, this is dumb, and it's dishonest, and it'd be better if he were upfront and didn't make up stories in his head, but still he lets it continue on.

Maggie puts her hand on his shoulder. "Seriously though, what's wrong?"

He shrugs. "Walt's cool."

"Not him. I'm worried about you, Reggie."

Reggie says, "Oh."

Maggie kisses him on the forehead and asks him if he wants to go home.

Reggie says, "It's your party," which it is; it's Maggie's graduation party. She's just graduated from art school. Transportation Design. It's kind of a big deal, but she says, "I don't really care for parties."

Then this guy named Khalil comes over and starts talking to Maggie. Reggie just met Khalil. Khalil also went to art school, graduated the year before. Fine Art. Reggie watches them talk. The two of them look nice together. Maggie is tall and Khalil is tall. Reggie wonders if people think he has a hang-up about being short. He honestly doesn't have any issues about being short. It's not even that he's so short. It's just that he's not tall.

Reggie says, "I'm gonna get another beer."

Maggie and Khalil don't seem to hear him. He doesn't get another beer. He goes outside instead to have a cigarette. He doesn't have to go outside to smoke. There are people smoking inside, but he goes outside anyway. As he goes through the door to the backyard, he sees Hanna. She's not with anyone. He stops and watches her. She's smoking. She has a can of cola that she's using as an ashtray. She's holding the can in her one hand and her cigarette in the other. She looks over. They make eye contact. Reggie gets nervous. He almost turns to walk back into the house, but Hanna calls his name.

"Chiang," she says. "We keep finding each other."

Reggie says, "Divine intervention."

He's embarrassed for saying that but also proud, because he's not usually good at banter. Not that this is banter, but it's something like banter.

Hanna says, "What are the odds?"

Reggie should say something clever to keep the banter going, something about the odds actually being very high, but he can't think of a clever way to say it. Hanna doesn't say anything clever back either. She just asks him if he came out to smoke. He nods. She offers him a cigarette. He takes it. She lights it. They smoke. They stand and smoke for a while. Then Reggie asks if Hanna wants another drink.

"No thanks. I'm thinking of going home."

"Where's home?"

"Main and Maine."

Main and Maine is on the other side of town.

Reggie says, "I can give you a ride."

Reggie doesn't have a car, but he has the keys to Maggie's.

"That's okay. I don't mind walking."

"It's too far to walk. Let me drive you."

Hanna seems to think about it for a second and then says, "Sure."

Reggie and Hanna leave the party without telling anyone and set out in the direction of the beach. They're not planning to go to the actual beach. They just drive that way down the main street. The main street is actually called Main Street. It goes east-west from the highway to the beach. Along the way are twenty or so north-south streets that cross Main. These streets are Avenues and named after states. They start with Hawaii Avenue and end with Maine Avenue. So, at the end, it's Main and Maine.

Main Street is busy in the daytime, but it's nighttime. So, it's quiet now. It's still a slow drive because of the many stop signs. It's not late though. Places are open. They stop at the stop sign on Ohio, next to the Ohio Ave Coffee Shop.

Hanna says, "You ever been to that place?"

Reggie says, "Yeah, you should try it."

"Oh, yeah, no. I've been there."

"Oh," says Reggie. "The donuts are good."

Hanna turns to him and says, "I could eat."

Reggie turns onto Ohio and parks the car. He and Hanna then go into the coffee shop. It's an old-fashioned kind of coffee shop. It has a waitress, a little jukebox at the table, and all-day breakfast food. It's the kind of coffee shop where old people go to be nostalgic, but Reggie and Hanna are not old people so they don't feel nostalgic there. They are the youngest people there. They're also the only Asian people there. Reggie notices this and mentions it.

Hanna says, "You have a lot of preoccupations."

Reggie says, "I don't know if I do."

Reggie guesses she's waiting for him to say more. He doesn't say anything more.

"What's up with you, Chiang? I wonder."

She says that as if she is psychoanalyzing him. He asks if she's a psychology major. She says that she was, she graduated two years ago. Reggie didn't know that. She doesn't ask him what his major is, but maybe she already knows.

They sit and eat their donuts and drink their coffee. They're both quiet for a while. Reggie finishes his coffee. Hanna waves the waitress over. The waitress refills his cup and asks Hanna if she wants more. Hanna says no thank you. She then starts to tell Reggie stories. Reggie thinks they're going to be wild party stories, but they aren't wild party stories. They are stories about back home. Back home for Hanna is Houston. Reggie didn't know she was from Houston. She talks about the church in Houston where she grew up in, how much she liked it, and then how she dated the youth pastor.

"His name was Mark," she says. "He was like thirty, and I was still in high school. The whole thing messed me up for years. Maybe that's why I left Texas, but who can know for sure."

Reggie says, "California is better."

Hanna says, "California isn't so great either. People in California are duplicitous. You all act like you're easy-going but you're actually obsessed with social hierarchy."

Then she says that she's sorry. Then she pauses and says, "I can tell that you're different."

Reggie has lost track of the conversation. Hanna looks at him and frowns a little bit. Not like she's mad at him. He can tell from her eyes. Her eyes aren't mad. It's more like she's a little bit sad. He thinks it's maybe the way he's staring at her.

She says, "I feel like I can tell you things."

Reggie nods. Hanna shifts in her seat a little, tilting her head like she's trying to get a better look at Reggie.

She says, "Did something bad happen to you when you were little?"

Reggie is not expecting this question.

He says, "What do you mean?"

"You're kind of hypervigilant."

"I don't know what that means."

"It's trauma theory. Hypervigilance. It's a trauma response. It means something terrible happened to you, and now you're always on the lookout for danger."

"I don't think anything bad has happened to me."

"Well. It's just a theory."

Reggie expects her to reach out her hand and take his hand because that seems like something someone would do in this situation if this were a movie. But she doesn't do that. This is not a movie. Instead, Hanna takes a sip of water.

Reggie sighs. It's not like a sigh that's trying to communicate something. It's just an exhale.

Hanna says, "That whole thing with Mark messed me up. Not just because of him, but because people found out, and then it was like everybody either wanted to save me or take advantage of me."

She laughs a kind of a tired laugh, and then continues, "I don't know. Maybe that's how it is all the time for girls, for women. You know?"

Reggie doesn't think that's true, but he's never thought

about it. He's never thought about what it's like all the time for girls, for women.

He says, "I've never thought about it."

She says, "No, of course not."

He's trying to listen, but he's not, not really. He's mostly just listening to the sound of her voice. It's a pretty voice. It's like a song. Hanna's voice is like a song where the words don't matter, you just like the song. It could be about death or peanut butter or anything, and you wouldn't care. It just sounds good to you.

She says, "I know I didn't really love Mark. It was an illusion. He tricked me. But I also tricked myself, you know? Have you ever felt that way?"

"Yes," says Reggie. "Yes, I think so."

He doesn't say anything else right away. So, Hanna keeps talking about Mark. Reggie wonders what Mark looks like. He wonders if he's white or if he's Asian or Black or something else. He thinks Mark must be thirty-five now. He wonders if he looks young for his age or if he just looks his actual age.

Hanna says, "That's one reason I like Walt. Walt's so obvious. You know what I mean? He's just what he is. No tricks."

It takes Reggie a second to remember who Walt is. Then he also remembers Maggie. He remembers them both in a past tense way. Like they're people he used to know from a way's back.

Reggie says, "Yeah."

He then stares into Hanna's eyes. He does this thing that his cousin told him about, the soul stare. He gives Hanna the soul stare. He's not sure he's doing it right. He stares at Hanna's left eye with his left eye. It's supposed to have something to do with the hunter-gatherer instinct. It doesn't seem to be working, but he keeps at it.

Hanna says, "You okay, Chiang?"

Reggie looks away. "I'm okay. I was just looking at your eyes. It's just your eyes are so green."

Hanna takes a napkin out of the dispenser. She wipes her nose with the napkin. She looks up at him and tilts her head forward. Reggie leans forward too.

She says, "They're just contacts."

Hanna dabs at her eyes with the edges of her napkin. Reggie gets his wallet out and puts ten dollars on the table.

After the coffee shop, Hanna says that she can walk the rest of the way. Reggie asks if she's sure, and she says, yes, it's just a couple blocks. Then he asks if she wants him to walk with her. She doesn't say yes or no, so Reggie leaves the car and the two of them walk around for a while. They go a couple streets down to Virginia Avenue. There they walk through Olde Farmers Market, which is really more like an outdoor shopping mall. It's closed. They walk around it. It's made to look like a barn. It has weathered wood panels and farm relics like rusted fittings and wagon wheels. There are stores for pie and toffee. Also, there is a jewelry store. Hanna stops there. Reggie stops too. They look at the display through the glass. The jewelry is put away. The only things left are things used to show off the jewelry, the display trees and manikin busts.

Past the stores, they get to the petting zoo. They lean on the gates and try to see the animals. They can see some of the animals. They're far away. Hanna points to a group of pigs sleeping and tells Reggie to listen to them snore. There are maybe five of them. They are fitted together like jigsaw pieces. Reggie listens for snoring, but he doesn't hear anything. One pig, who is on the outside of the group, nuzzles its way into the middle. The other pigs make room for it. They don't seem to wake up.

Hanna puts her arm through Reggie's arm, at the elbow. She rests her head on his shoulder. Reggie looks at the pigs. He looks at Hanna. She's closed her eyes. He closes his eyes too.

After the zoo is a playground on New York, off Main by a half block. The playground is on the other side of a park, a nice park, with very big trees and an artificial creek that runs through it. They get to the playground and stand by the swings. Hanna sits on one and starts swinging, just a little bit. Reggie is just standing there, but when it seems like they might be staying for a while, he goes ahead and sits on a swing too. It feels strange to him, sitting on a swing. He hasn't sat on a swing since he was little, which seems like a long time ago. He wonders why he hasn't. He wonders why more adults don't.

The two of them swing. Reggie swings higher than Hanna. It's not because he's trying to. It's because of the length of the chains. Reggie tries to swing lower, so that they can even out, but this doesn't seem to work. He gives up and tries to just enjoy the swinging. He likes the feeling. It's a little bit queasy because he's been drinking, but it's good. He doesn't feel it in his head. He feels it in his stomach. The feeling in his stomach is like fear but also like happiness. The feeling of swinging goes well with the feeling of being with Hanna.

From the darkness, Reggie hears someone yell something.

He can't make out what it is. He turns his head to where it came from. He doesn't see anyone.

When their swings pass, he says, "Did you hear that?"

Hanna doesn't answer. She lunges forward. He hears the yelling again. The voice says, "Drop the zero!"

Reggie doesn't know what that means. He looks over again. Two guys are walking up to them. They're athletic looking guys. They look kind of like Walt. They're not Walt though. They just look like the kind of guy Walt looks like. White guys. Sports guys. They're both wearing tank tops and basketball shorts. They look like they came from the gym, except that they also look like they're drunk. The one who's talking is wearing a baseball cap with a B on the front, for Boston maybe, or maybe for Bruins, which could still be for Boston. Reggie is not sure why he is trying to figure this out.

The B-hat guy says, "Drop the zero!"

Reggie still doesn't understand. Hanna keeps swinging. She seems like she doesn't hear them, or is trying to ignore them.

The B-hat guy walks out in front of Reggie, in front of the swings. He stands just out of reach of Reggie's feet. Reggie has to bend his knees so that he doesn't kick him. The other guy goes behind them. He's shorter than the B-hat guy and skinnier. Reggie cranes his neck to try to see him. He's standing behind Hanna.

The skinnier guy says, "Hey, you need a push?"

Then he pushes her.

Hanna says, "What the fuck. No, I do not want a push."

The skinnier guy laughs.

The B-hat guy says, "Drop the zero and get with the hero."

He says this in a sing-song voice, like it's from a kid's poem. He leans to the left and points his thumb at Reggie and nods at the skinnier guy. They both laugh. Reggie figures out that in this situation, Reggie is the zero and the B-hat guy is the hero. Then the B-hat guy looks at Hanna. She swings forward. He curls his right arm in a muscle man pose. Reggie can see his bicep bulging even in the dark. Hanna swings backwards. The skinnier guy laughs and pushes her again.

She says, "Dude, leave me alone."

The B-hat guy laughs more. "Ah, don't be mad. We're being nice. We like you. We wanna be friends."

Hanna swings forward again and jumps off the swing. Reggie wants to jump off too, but the B-hat guy is in his way. Hanna lands in the sand and trips over the B-hat guy's foot. She stumbles and hits her knee on the concrete walkway. Reggie is still swinging. It seems really, very stupid for him to be still swinging. But there he is.

The skinnier guy walks over toward Hanna. The B-hat guy also takes a step toward her. It's finally clear for Reggie to jump. Reggie jumps off.

The B-hat guy leans over Hanna, "Oh no, you got an owie."

She says, "I'm fine."

He says, "No, you're bleeding. Hold up. I have Band-Aids."

He reaches into his pocket. He takes out a Band-Aid. It's weird that he has a Band-Aid in his pocket.

Hanna says, "No, thank you."

He says, "Come on."

She says, "No."

She then takes Reggie's arm, and they start walking away. Reggie doesn't say anything. They keep walking. The B-hat guy walks next to them. He keeps pace with them. Reggie doesn't look at him. Reggie looks ahead. The B-hat guy stops. Reggie and Hanna keep walking. They walk faster. Reggie is walking very fast. Hanna pulls her arm free and takes Reggie's hand and pulls it down. Reggie pulls his hand away, but he slows down. They keep walking. The B-hat guy yells out one more time, "Drop the zero!" He says this with enthusiasm. He sustains the last two syllables. The Zeeee Rowww.

Reggie and Hanna walk the next couple minutes or so in silence, passing the last few avenues, Massachusetts and then Vermont. Reggie is upset, but he doesn't have the words to express it. Instead, he stares out into the space in front of him. He breathes through his nose. He clenches and unclenches his fists.

Hanna asks him if he is okay. He shrugs and doesn't answer.

She says, "Do you want to call the cops? Maybe we should call the cops. I'll call them."

Reggie doesn't think they should call the cops. He doesn't think it's a good idea. He feels worse even thinking about calling the cops. He feels like acid is in his veins. He feels both hot and cold. He thinks he should go back. He wants to go back. He feels like he should go back and do something, or at least, go back and say something. He tries to think of something to say. The things he thinks of to say are terrible. He thinks he should tell those guys to fuck themselves, or to fuck each other, or their mothers, or their fathers. He thinks he should tell them that their fathers are fucking them and that's why they're such giant assholes.

Hanna takes his hand again and says, "Hey, it's okay."

He looks at her, and for a second, he's mad at her, but he forces himself not to be. Then Hanna tries to make a joke out of it. She says something about the B-hat guy's line, "Get with the hero? How lame is that?"

Reggie tries to agree with her, but he doesn't feel like that line was lame. He feels like he himself is lame, and he feels like the B-hat guy's line is true. The B-hat guy is the hero, and Reggie is the zero.

Then they reach Maine Avenue, and it's only ten o'clock, but it seems later. Everything is black, but the kind of black that moves and has shape. The sand, the sky, the water.

They stop at the end of the sidewalk, at the start of the sand. Hanna lets go of Reggie's hand. Reggie takes her hand back. She tries to pull her hand away, but he holds on. He then leans in and kisses her. It's not more than a second before he realizes she's not at all reciprocating. He stops and lets her go and she steps off the path and on to the sand and looks up at Reggie and then exhales a long breath out.

She says, "What are you doing, Reggie?"

He says, "I'm sorry."

She says, "Why are guys so fragile?"

Reggie is not sure what she's talking about, if she's talking about those two guys at the park or something else.

Reggie says, "What do you mean?"

She doesn't answer. It's quiet. It's dark. Reggie can't tell for sure, but it looks like she might be crying or about to cry.

He says, "What's going on?"

She says, "You know, I was scared too. I was mad too. It wasn't just you. I was there too."

She puts a hand to her face, rubbing her eyes and breathing

loudly, like she has a lot more to say but doesn't know if she can say it without things getting ugly. Reggie doesn't know what's happening. He tries to apologize again, though he's not sure what for. Hanna seems to know that he doesn't know what he's apologizing for.

She says, "Why are you all like this?"

"Who are you talking about?" he says.

Then the ocean makes a low rumbling sound. Hanna turns away from Reggie, turning her ear to the ocean, as if it's speaking to her. She then starts walking on the sand toward the water.

Reggie is still on the concrete. He watches her. He thinks, she's got it all wrong. He's not the villain here. Why would she think that? He is obviously not the villain here. He's the good guy. Or at least he's the regular guy. The regular guy, at least, and definitely not the bad guy.

He then also steps off the concrete onto the sand and starts to follow her toward the water. She walks ahead of him. She doesn't talk to him or look back at him. She just keeps going and the gap between them starts to widen. He asks her to wait, to slow down. He asks her to wait for him. He speeds up. He tries to catch up to her, but she stays ahead.

"Wait," he says, "Hanna, please."

He then tries to speed up even more, but it feels like it's too late, and even though it doesn't seem like she's trying to get away from him, he cannot catch her.

A PENNY SHORT

I ask the casino waitress how to work the slot machine. I think she looks like me, even in her ornate navy-blue bikini top and train conductor's hat. But still, she's Asian and she's my age. She's tall too, taller than me, and I'm already tall for an Asian girl. I ask again, sister to sister, about the machine. She nods her head. I don't know what she means by that. I ask her for cigarettes. She tells me she's all out. I can see cigarettes right there in her box. I ask her for a gin and tonic. This she agrees to with another nod.

"Okay. Be right back with that."

I watch her walk toward the bar. She stops several times to check in with other gamblers. I lose her in the crowd. I'm left staring at my penny slot machine. A Penny for Your Thoughts, it's called. It's got five reels and like twenty different symbols on each reel. I have no idea how to win on this thing. I've tried every way I can imagine. I've put the max bet. I've put the minimum bet. I've pulled the arm. I've pushed the button. I've said a prayer. I've closed my eyes. And every time, I get some outcome I don't understand telling me I've done a little better or a little worse.

The guys would say I'm wasting my time, that the game is rigged against the player. The guys meaning Rick Junior and Lincoln, the other two players in our string trio. Junior is the violist and current boyfriend—or fiancé, technically. Lincoln is the violinist and ex-boyfriend, also technically. I left them both at the wedding reception. The best man was toasting the groom by listing all the women he'd given up for his new bride, and I'd had about enough. But Junior seemed into it. Taking notes, maybe, for our upcoming wedding. And there was Lincoln getting loaded on free liquor. He'd looked at me with those drunken, red eyes and asked me to stay. I said I had to go. We both shrugged, and that was that.

I'm sure they're probably looking for me by now. Not that I'm hiding. I've been sitting here at Penny for Your Thoughts for God knows how long. Time measured in pennies is hard to track. But now it seems I've only got one penny left. I look at it a moment, kiss it for good luck. It tastes like tea. In one motion I drop it into my machine and pull the lever.

Just then, three guys I recognize from the wedding pass through the end of the row. They're young and lean and wearing tailored suits. The best-looking one stops and waves at me, and I wave back with this conditioned cheerfulness.

He mimes the air cello and shouts, "Hey, Yoyo Ma! You were amazing."

I wave again, still smiling, a little more authentically now.

He gives me a thumbs up and makes his way toward me.

I say, "Yoyo Ma's a dude, but thank you."

He laughs.

"No," he says. "Seriously. I'm not being ironic. That was like truly superior."

The other two nod in agreement. Then they all keep walking, past me down the aisle and out the other end. I turn back to my machine: Bet 1, Winner Paid 0.

And that's it for my gambling career, and that waitress still hasn't come back. I stand up to look for her but she's nowhere to be seen. While I'm standing, an old white lady comes and sits down at what was my machine. I sit down at the machine next to me. This one's called The Penny Pincher and has a white-gloved Mickey Mouse hand pinching a golden penny as its graphic.

I ask the old lady for a cigarette.

She says, "You should ask the waitress."

I say, "I did. She doesn't seem to like me."

"It's nothing personal. They just work slow to make you gamble more."

"That's funny. Because, actually, I'm not gambling."

I show her my empty coin bucket. The old lady eyes the bucket and shakes her head, sighing. She fishes her hand into her penny cup and starts taking coins out one at a time. She carefully counts each penny out loud, twenty-two of them. She hands them to me in a neat little stack.

"Play until these run out, then go home. You need rest."

I tell her she's right, and then I pump all twenty-two pennies into my machine and pull the handle. The reels land one after another, kuh-thunk, kuh-thunk- kuh-thunk, and it looks like I might have won something. I look to the old lady, hoping she'll corroborate my excitement, but she doesn't. I look back at The Penny Pincher, the gloved cartoon hand clutching its riches just out of my reach.

The old lady says, "Sorry, dear."

I shrug.

"Hey, can I ask you something?"

She nods.

I say, "So, I got this job offer."

I try to smile big and exude a bit of pride. I think that I should feel proud. I should feel about this job like how I felt about cello, when things were going well. How I felt about Sunderman, and how I felt about subbing at Annapolis and The National and at U of M. How I beat the odds. A poor kid raised by a single mom, but I was talented, so talented! And I was a worker. I was a worker once. I'd spent my childhood in more practice hours than sleep, each minute like an optimistic coin dropped into a slot machine.

I think I should feel like that about this job. But I don't.

I go on.

"It's good money. I mean really good, like Lexuses and no debts good. And it's easy. I mean, it's not easy, just more certain, a lot more certain, you know? I'd be selling real estate, but not even real real estate, but like a real estate mutual fund, like if real estate were stocks, something like that. I don't know. I'm not sure I really get it. But it's sort of the family business, except not exactly my family. It's Junior's family. Junior's my boyfriend. He's here, somewhere. He's gonna want to know what I plan to do. I want to know too, what I want to do, about the job, about cello, about him. Jesus, I don't know what I want to do. I just need like some set of instructions, you know, like a signal, an omen even."

The old lady says, "Well."

She says this, then pauses, as if taking in the gravity of my question, making sure that she gives me the best possible wisdom because God knows this could be the turning point in my life.

She continues, "Well, having some security does sound nice."

"Yeah," I say.

I don't look up. I just watch the wheels on Penny for Your Thoughts spin.

I think about what Lincoln told me, that life is only about what you do, not who you are. There is no you, he once said in a moment of drug-induced clarity. So then, if I do good, I am good. If I play cello, I am a cellist. If I sell real estate, I am a real estate seller.

Or is Lincoln wrong, and really it's who I am in my heart that counts. It doesn't matter if I have the wrong job or marry the wrong person or never play the cello again, as long as I still love the things I love, deep down.

The old lady says, "Pretty girl."

She pinches me on the cheek.

Then she pulls the lever on her machine, what was formerly my machine. The music starts. It's jangly and almost has a melody to it, like the intro to a children's song. A bunch of random symbols come up on her reels, one at a time, landing with an amplified clunk. The finished outcome doesn't look like anything to me, though I can barely focus, so who knows. It looks like elephants, queens, and exclamation points. The old lady gasps and the machine lights up and bells start to ring. She starts clapping her hands and shouting.

"Doggone it, doggone it, doggone it!"

The casino waitress, the one that's been ignoring me, comes over to the old lady and gives her a big hug. Then a Latina woman in a black suit comes over and shakes the old lady's hand. I don't know exactly how it happened, but I think this old lady just got rich. She's just won a lot of money. Not just like a couple grand, like a regular jackpot, but like the progressive, like a million bucks or something. I'm sitting there watching them take the old lady's picture, and it all feels like the punchline out of a TV sitcom.

I try to smile at her, but I can't bring myself to do it. I elbow her, vying for her attention. She puts a soft hand on my elbow and moves away from me. I keep trying to make eye contact so that maybe she'll notice me.

"Hey," I say. "That was my machine."

The old lady says, "A day late and a penny short."

There is not even the tiniest bit of remorse in her voice.

In all the commotion, I don't notice all the people that have come over to see what's going on. Junior is among them.

Junior grabs me by the shoulders.

"Lucky," he says.

He calls me Lucky. I've asked him not to, but he won't stop.

"Where have you been? I've been looking all over for you."

I look up at him, bleary-eyed.

"Hey, babe," I say. "Just playing my slots, you know. Pennies for Penny."

My name is Penny. In case that wasn't clear.

"What? What's wrong with you? Are you okay?"

"I'm good," I say. "I am."

He grabs at my hand, not grab-grab, but more like gently takes my hand. I let him. I look at him and ask if he'll get me some smokes and a drink.

I say, "Gin and tonic."

He hands me his cigarettes.

"Gin and tonic?"

I shrug and say, "Yeah. Why not."

He leaves for the bar. Before he turns the corner, I'm up, shaking out the cobwebs, blinking repeatedly until I spot the old lady. She's walking with the woman in the black suit. They go through a door, a very regular looking door with a small brass plaque that says: Office. It's seems like an odd place to hand over a million dollars, but what do I know.

I head toward them, passing the other penny slots: A Penny Earned—A Penny Saved, Pennies from Heaven, The Penny Jar, Lucky Penny. I stop at Lucky Penny, two-thirds of the way to the office door. I light a cigarette, wondering what I'm doing. What exactly do I think I'm doing now. I stand there. I smoke. It seems like forever. I see the casino waitress, that same one. She's got the same box around her neck, those same cigarettes that she doesn't want to give me. She passes those same three guys from the wedding. My number-one fan, the guy who'd waved at me earlier, is now shouting something at the waitress. But she doesn't stop. Maybe she doesn't hear him. She walks by, a few quick steps with her head high, and then I see the guy give a series of pelvic thrusts to the space behind her back. His companions slap and laugh, raising their champagne flutes in a toast to truth and courage and all good things lost in our postmodern age.

I wonder if this waitress and these guys and the old lady and Junior and Lincoln and me, even me, are all secretly good people, amazing and bright, just waiting for some angel to tap us on the shoulder and wake us. Or maybe we are the angels, and we're the ones looking for some lost human soul to knead and shape, or to defeat decisively like that thing from the deep that played the wrestler's sinews like strings on a harp . . .

Jesus, I don't know.

The old lady comes out of the office, a small packet of forms in her hands. The woman in the suit shakes her hand again. The old lady smiles and says something. Then she turns to walk out the casino doors. I watch, balancing an invisible scale in my head, contemplating difficult answers to imaginary questions. I watch for another second and then follow.

KOREAN JESUS

When I finally find Korean Jesus, I can tell who he is right
away. I can tell he's Korean because of his face and also because of his accent, but the Jesus part I don't get until after
listening to him preach for a while.

It's late summer, Tuesday night, early evening, Central Park,
Pasadena, California. It's hot. The hottest day of the year so
far. It's looking to stay hot all night. I'm hot. I'm standing in
the sun. I'm wearing long pants and a sport coat. I have the
coat on for fashion, but also because I've got something under
my coat that I don't want anybody else to see. Jesus is in the
sun too. It doesn't look like the heat is bothering him. He's sitting at a concrete park bench. It's not really a bench but more
like a picnic table. It's a picnic table with benches connected
to it. Two benches connected to it, one on each side.

There are twenty, twenty-one people with him, mostly
white, or actually about fifty-fifty white and Asian. Most
of them are standing. Six are sitting at the table with Jesus.
They're all young. Except for Jesus. Jesus looks older, like thir-
ty-something or forty even. Older than me, and I'm already

older than most of the crowd here. Most of the crowd here looks young. They're dressed in what looks like beachwear: board shorts and swimsuit tops or tank tops, sunglasses, visors, stuff like that. Some of the men not even wearing a shirt. Jesus is sitting in the middle of everyone. He's preaching. It's like a monologue. Like he's giving a lecture, but casual.

Jesus says: This all starts when you're little, like really little, too little to understand consequences.

Somebody says: How old?

Some other people laugh when that person yells out, how old. Jesus laughs too.

Jesus says: How old? Oh dang. Come on. I mean, I don't know. It's not like a specific number. It's just little.

Jesus puts his hand out in front of himself to sort of show how tall of a kid he's talking about. The people around the table nod.

Jesus says: When you're still little like that, we come around to each of you and ask you what you want. And whatever it is you wish for right then, we do it.

The people around the table laugh.

Jesus says: I'm being serious here, you guys. Totally serious. Every kid, when they're little, gets one wish, and whatever that wish is, we grant it. And I mean whatever it is. Anything. Whatever it is that they want right then.

The people around the table laugh again. Jesus laughs too. But it's not the kind of laugh to show that he's just joking around. It's the kind of laugh to show how this whole thing could potentially get really fucked up.

Jesus says: You can probably guess what something like 80 percent of the wishes are.

Somebody says: Candy.

Somebody Else says: Toys.

A Third Person says: Puppies.

Jesus says: Puppies? Who said puppies?

The person who said puppies raises her hand. Jesus gets up halfway from his seat and reaches out his hand. The person who said puppies doesn't seem to know what he wants. Jesus motions for her to come closer. She comes closer. Then Jesus gives her a hard high-five. The high-five makes a loud slap sound. The person who said puppies rubs her hand like it really stings.

Jesus says: There you go! Puppies! Little kids love puppies. Fluffy, downy, googly-eyed puppies. Who can blame them. Right? Can I get an amen?

Everybody says amen. Even I say amen. Everyone says amen right away except for this guy next to me. He doesn't say amen right away. Then he suddenly says amen after everybody else says amen. It just comes out. It's awkward and real loud. The people around him look at him like they're mad or judgmental, or maybe just surprised.

Without thinking too much about it, I reach out and pat the guy who didn't say amen on the back, like a friendly pat. A chummy pat. Like how you'd pat somebody on the back to show them that you appreciate them, like they'd just done something that you appreciate. He sort of drops his head a little bit and smiles as if to show me that he appreciates me too, that he appreciates the pat on the back. Then Jesus goes on.

Jesus says: So, all those 80 percent of wishes. Let's call them puppy-wishes. All those puppy-wishes, we just go ahead and do it. We don't even think about it, we just go ahead and do it. But . . .

Then Jesus pauses and looks around. It's almost 8:00 p.m. but it's still one hundred degrees out, maybe more. It's still light out too. Mostly light. Just a little bit dark. Jesus can see everybody. Everybody can see everybody else. We can all see Jesus.

Jesus says: It's the other 20 percent though. That's when things get sketchy. Because we still have to grant their wishes. Whatever it is. Even if it's, excuse my French, but even if it's really jacked up. We still do it.

Some of the people gasp out loud like they're cartoon characters. I laugh. Then pretty fast I stop laughing because I realize they're not being sarcastic. They're really gasping because this is really scary to them.

Jesus says: Yeah. You know it. I mean, sometimes these little kids, bless their hearts, they don't know any better. How can they? That's the whole point. If they knew better, it'd be too late to give them their wishes. So, they don't. They don't know any better.

The crowd starts shifting around and grumbling. Some of them are whispering to each other under their breath like muttering. Jesus raises his hands like to have everybody settle down.

Jesus says: Okay, okay. Don't freak out. Don't let your imaginations get carried away. It's not some kind of sociopathic stuff. It's not kids wishing for people dead! Come on! Is that what you guys are thinking? Little kids wishing their dads or baby brothers to drop dead or their moms or their teachers? No!

There's a kind of collective sigh of relief. Then there's a little bit more rumbling. People are getting restless. They're probably getting restless because this thing is going kind of long and also, it's just so hot out. I shift around. I'm sweating all over. I wipe my forehead with my coat sleeve. I pull at my waistband. My waistband is especially uncomfortable and sweaty because I've got a gun tucked in there. I want to take the gun out, but I can't because I don't want to alarm anybody. So, I leave the gun there. But it's not at all comfortable.

Jesus says: No, no, no, I mean, I'm just saying, there's some bad people out there. I sometimes wish these kids would just go ahead and wish them dead. But they don't. They're still little. Too little for justice, unfortunately. And you get it, right? I say unfortunately because it'd really make everybody's life a lot easier if we could just get rid of a bunch of the bad guys right then and there. You know what I mean?

Some people nod in agreement. I don't nod because I'm not really sure I agree. It might seem like I would agree or that I should agree, and it's not that I disagree. I just don't know for sure if I agree.

Jesus lets us all think about this for a couple more seconds. Then he starts up again.

Jesus says: Okay, okay. All right, folks. Okay. So, let me tell you a story. An illustrative kind of story. It's what us preachermen call An Illustration. And this illustration is a true story. A true story of a kid I know. A man named Reginald, Reggie for short. A sweet kid. A sweet, sad, kinda scared little kid. Can I tell you Reggie's story?

Jesus looks right at me when he says this. I feel weird. I feel really weird because my name is Reginald. Also, I go by

Reggie for short. But he can't mean me. I don't know Jesus. I mean, I know who he is, but I don't really know him. So, I don't see how he can mean me when I don't even know him.

Jesus says: This is Reggie's story. But I want you guys to think about it as if it's your own. Because even though this story is just an illustration, you might come to see that the point of any illustration is this: That when you really think about, the story, the illustration, is really about you.

〜

II. THE ILLUSTRATION

The Illustration goes like this: There's a little orphan kid named Reginald, or Reggie for short. Reggie wasn't always an orphan though. Reggie starts out with his parents. Then his mom dies. He doesn't know much about how she dies. The little bit that he does know is that his mom and dad had been fighting and then something happens and then his mom dies. That's all Reggie knows. But the fact is Reggie's mom and dad fought a lot. They fought a lot and most all their fights were about the same thing. Most all their fights were about affairs. And by affairs, I mean infidelity. That last fight, the last fight before his mom dies, is about Reggie's mom having had an infidelity with their local church preacher. Reggie doesn't remember that. He's too little. But that's what that last fight is about.

So, as it goes, after his mom dies, Reggie's dad leaves and he never sees his dad again, at least as far as I know, he never sees his dad again. And Reggie's alone. Not completely alone. He stays with people, family members, his grandfather, I think, adopts him or something like that. So, Reggie isn't literally, physically alone, but in his heart, he feels it. That aloneness. In his heart. He feels it.

Reggie especially feels it when the people around him are arguing, fighting. Doesn't matter what the fight is about. Reggie feels this terrible bad, nervous feeling in his stomach and, strangely, in his arms, like his arms go cold and tingly. But he never says anything, because he doesn't know what to say or who to say it to. Reggie doesn't know what to say because he doesn't understand why he feels like that, but you and I might have an idea. Because you and I might understand that Reggie's in kind of a vulnerable situation. He's an orphan. His mom's dead. His dad's gone. He's living out some kind of Oedipal nightmare from his proverbial preverbal childhood. Some kind of existential insecurity that he's too little to have the executive functioning to process . . .

Sorry, that got a little heady, but you all understand.

So, Reggie's just this ball of nerves. Just nervous and not knowing what to do about it. Stomach hurts. Arms cold. Feet and legs cold too. Head hurts. Not hurts so much as feels like he can't think, like his head can't get organized. Reggie doesn't understand why this all is happening to him. He feels like a crazy person. A crazy person pacing around the house. Not saying anything. Not knowing what to say. Just pacing around.

That's when we all come around.

We say: Reggie?

Reggie looks at us. He looks surprised to see us.

We say: What is it in your heart of hearts that you most wish for right now?

Reggie rubs the eyes on his little face.

Reggie says: I don't know.

We say: You can just say it.

Reggie says: I don't like people fighting.

We say: You want to make people not fight?

Reggie says: Yes.

We say: Why do you want to make people not fight?

Reggie says: Because it scares me.

It's sad to hear Reggie say this, but you probably wouldn't be surprised to hear that a lot of little kids say something like this. Sad, right?! So many kids scared of their parents fighting, just not feeling safe in that kind of environment. I mean, think about it! These little kids, so vulnerable. Their very lives at the mercy of their parents, or their parental substitutes.

So, so many kids have this same wish. So many that we made a protocol around how to grant this wish. The thing we do, and this is gonna make perfect sense when you hear it, the thing we do is we give these sweet little kids a kind of a super power. A gift. A talent. We give them this special talent where we turn them into a kind of an emotional firefighter. We make it so these kids are always looking out for fire, emotional fire. Listening in, checking your face, your voice, your posture, all of that, so they can figure out how you're feeling. Then they figure out if you're upset and they jump right in with firehoses and CPR, but you understand, it's not firehoses, it's more like smiles and back pats. It's smiles and back pats and everything's all okay. I mean, all okay as far as that kind of thing is okay.

This is the thing we do for kids like Reggie. We don't ask him if he's sure. We never do that. We just ask him what he wishes for and then we just give it to him. That's the deal. And by that we abide.

⮎

III. THE HIGHLIGHT

One of the people sitting next to Jesus takes out a guitar and starts playing. She plays a song by a popular folk-rock band, not their most popular song, but another song that I don't remember the name of. I try to figure out the name of the song, but I can't figure it out. I'm a big fan of that band, but I can't remember the name of that song. It's like my head's having a hard time organizing my thoughts. I rub my eyes. I hum along to the song. The people at the table sing along. Some of the standing people also sing along. One guy has a little basket that he carries around. Some people put money in the basket. He tells the people who don't put money that he's got a swipe thing for credit cards.

Jesus stays seated. He lifts his hands up and sways to the music. This all goes on for maybe a minute or maybe less and then the guitar player plays a sort of wrap-up riff and Jesus starts talking again.

Jesus says: Ok, friends. Let's wrap this up. Let's get to The Highlight of my message, okay? The Highlight. The Point. The Moral of the story, so to speak. So, this is it. This is The Highlight.

Everybody starts to settle down. Jesus waits for them to get organized. They redirect their attention back to Jesus.

Jesus says: So, this wish that we grant. This wish we grant

for whatever it is that you want when you're still little. That wish. That wish is not the end of it.

People seem to get a little energized now. Maybe because they can tell this thing is almost over.

Jesus says: Because, that first wish, that first wish is almost always a mistake. Can you see what I mean? You always wish for the wrong thing, even though it seems like the right thing at the time. That's why we give you that wish when you're too little to know better. Not because then you'll wish for something good, but because we already know you'll wish for something bad, but you're still little, so at least you won't wish for something that's too, too jacked up, you see what I mean?

There are some people now with kind of confused looks on their faces.

Jesus says: We give you that first wish then, when you're still little so as to protect you from yourselves. But that is not when it ends. There is more. Am I right? There is always more.

Jesus slowly gets up from the bench. He steps back and stands up straight. As he stands up, we can all see how big he is. He's a big man. Very, very tall and also thick, strong looking. He looks like some kind of middle-aged Korean lumberjack surfer.

He starts talking again, but quieter now. Much quieter.

Jesus says: There's a second wish.

We all lean forward to hear him.

Jesus says: And this second wish only comes to a few, just a few, and by just a few, I mean those few who didn't wish for puppies and candy. I mean those few who wished for something else. Something desperate. Those are the few who sometimes come to be ready to be little again. You get

me? To be little again. To be innocent again. And the way we
know that they're ready is that they've used up that first wish.
They've used it all up. And it's kept them safe for a long, long
time. But all that time, they didn't know it, but all that time,
using that first wish, it was taking a toll on them. On their
bodies, on their minds, on their hearts. Wearing them out.
Using them up.

Jesus pauses and sort of takes a deep breath.

Jesus says: So, this second wish, when they get it, you want
to know what? Every single one who gets that second wish,
the thing is, they all wish for the same thing. The same thing.
They don't wish for money, even though most of the time they
could use it. They don't wish for revenge, even though most
of the time they want it. They don't even wish for the end of
poverty or the cure for cancer, even though those are good,
good, noble things. They don't even wish for that. Do you
want to know what each and every one of those that get a
second wish wish for?

Most everybody nods their heads, including me.

Jesus says: They wish for the only thing that really matters.
They wish for the only thing that ever really mattered. They
all wish to know what it feels like to be truly and completely,
unconditionally loved.

Right when he says that, I laugh out loud.

I say: Ha!

I say ha pretty loud, but nobody notices. Nobody notices except for the Amen Guy, the guy who said Amen at the
wrong time earlier and that I then patted on the back. That
guy notices. He looks at me and kind of nods. I nod back.
He waves at me. I wave back. He makes a kind of a motion

with his hands like he's pulling on the collar of an imaginary jacket.

Amen Guy mouths the words: Aren't you hot?

I shake my head.

I mouth the words: No, I'm okay.

The person with the guitar starts to play another song. This song is a song by a guy who was the singer in an old punk rock band. But this song is not a punk rock song. It's a pretty song called "Fields of Gold." I like that song. It's pretty, especially the way the person with the guitar sings it. I sort of get lost in the song for a second. The sun is setting and there is a kind of goldenness to everything. The people around Jesus start to bunch in closer. Some of them put their arms around each other. I think some of them are even crying. Actually, I'm sure of it. Some of them are definitely crying.

The Amen Guy starts to walk over to me. I look down and then look back up. He's still walking over to me. He waves at me. I wave back, but I also start to back away. He looks like a nice guy. I think he looks like a nice guy. But I still back away. He waves. It's a little kid wave. He waves a little kid wave and smiles at me. I nod back at him. I keep backing away.

Amen Guy mouths the words: Thank you.

I nod.

Amen Guy mouths the words: I'm glad you came.

I nod. I nod again. I back away. I then I turn and walk. I walk away, checking back until the Amen Guy stops looking at me. I'm just far enough so that it seems like I'm probably not there for the Jesus thing anymore. But I'm still close enough to see. I see Jesus. He makes his way through this little circle. He puts his hands on the Amen Guy. He puts his hands on the top of the head of the Amen Guy. He puts his hands on his shoulders. He puts his hands on the back of his neck. He leans in and says something to him. The Amen Guy gets emotional when Jesus does this. He starts crying and wraps his arms around Jesus. All the while, the guy with the credit card swipe and basket is going around.

〜

IV. THE PASSING OF THE PEACE

This ends after a short while. It's dusk now, still enough sunlight out to keep the streetlights from switching on. Most of the people leave. Jesus still hangs out. He talks to the two, three people who stay. He looks like he's praying. Then he's joking around. Then he's drinking a Diet Coke out of the can with a straw. When he's done with the Coke, he gets up from the bench and gives the few people left a hug and then starts to walk toward the street.

He walks toward a kind of fancy sports car that I don't know the name of. I follow him. He takes out the car remote and unlocks the car. I start running. I run toward him and his car. He doesn't see me running.

As he's getting in on the driver side, I open the passenger door and jump in too.

I'm sitting in the passenger seat. Jesus is sitting in the driver seat. He looks at me like he's not all that surprised. I grab my gun. I point my gun at him. He puts his hands up.

I try to say something, but I'm out of breath. I hold my hand up to him to signal for him to wait because I'm out of breath. He nods. I keep pointing the gun at him. He puts his hands down. I motion for him to put his hands back up. He puts his hands back up. I catch my breath.

I say: You fucked my wife.

Jesus says: I'm sorry. I'm not sure I know what you're talking about.

I say: You fucked my fuckin' wife, man!

Jesus keeps his hands up. He keeps his hands up and his eyes on me.

Jesus says: You're Genna's husband.

I say: Jenny! Jenny, not Genna. Jenny!

I rub my face, then I quickly stop rubbing my face. I point the gun at Jesus again.

I say: You fucked my wife.

Jesus says: Well, I didn't technically fuck her.

I shake the gun in his face. He doesn't seem to freak out about this. I shake it again

Jesus says: Okay. Let's just say I did make love to your wife.

I say: You fucked her.

Jesus says: I did not fuck her.

I say: The fuck you didn't.

I wave the gun around the car so as to say that I'm going to go crazy and shoot up Jesus and his fancy car.

Jesus says: I'm not trying to aggravate you. It's a necessary distinction. I didn't fuck Jenny. I didn't fuck her. I don't fuck people.

I say: What?

Jesus says: I don't fuck people.

I say: What?

Jesus says: I'm a virgin.

I'm about to say what again, but I don't. I think he's telling the truth. Then I think he's probably a really good liar. I say, fucking shit, and Jesus smiles and I don't know why, but I'm not so mad for a second. Then I picture this big, giant, old-ass, lumberjack Jesus having sex with Jenny, and I'm mad again.

I say: The fuck kind of name is Jesus?

Jesus says: It's my name. It's a very common Spanish name.

I say: You're Korean, man.

Jesus says: I'm Chinese actually.

I say: I thought you were Korean.

Jesus says: I get that a lot. Because of my face or because of my name?

I say: Name. But also face.

Jesus nods.

Jesus says: I'm glad you came today, Reggie.

I point the gun at him, really sticking it in his face now.

Jesus says: I'm sorry about your wife. But you gotta know, that's something that's been a long time coming. And you're gonna see, it's better this way. The two of you. Well, the two of you have run your course.

I don't know what to say about that.

Jesus says: What do you want, Reggie? What do you really want?

I say: I don't know.

Jesus says: You want my car? You seem to like my car.

I say: It is a nice car.

Jesus says: Okay. Let's say, I give you the car. But you sure that's what you really want?

I say: What are you doing, man! No, that's not what I said. I don't want your car.

I press the gun up against Jesus's forehead.

Jesus says: Is there something else then? What about revenge?

I keep the gun up against his head.

Jesus says: Or what about, I don't know, Jenny? You want Jenny back?

Jesus smiles. I think he's smiling because he's making a joke at me. But then I think he's not really making a joke at me. He's smiling because he's happy. I think that's what it is. He's smiling because he's happy.

My arm starts to get tired from holding up the gun, but I keep it held up, up to his forehead. He doesn't seem to mind though. He doesn't even seem to notice anymore that I have a gun to his head. He just smiles and looks at me. He looks me in the eyes. I can see his eyes. They're dark brown and kind of wet like he might start crying, but not the upset kind of crying, but the compassionate kind of crying.

He starts to lower his hands.

I say: Don't move.

I press the gun hard enough against his forehead to push his head back a little bit.

Jesus says: It's okay.

I say: Did Jenny tell you all that about me?

Jesus says: All what?

I say: All that in The Illustration.

Jesus says: Oh, I don't know. Probably. I got so many stories. It's hard to keep track where they come from. You know what I mean?

I sort of laugh, but my mouth doesn't work right so it comes out weird.

I say: Well, that is my story.

He nods. He nods like he understands. Like he understands that it's my story. Like that's the whole reason why he
told that story in the first place. The he goes on lowering his
hands. He lowers his hands until he's got his hands on my
shoulders. He's holding me by the shoulders. I shrug to get
him to let go of my shoulders, but his hands are really strong.

The radio in the car comes on. I don't know how Jesus got
the radio to come on, but it does. It comes on and there's a
song I don't know, but it's a pretty song. It sounds like the
"Hallelujah" song, but it's not. It's maybe the same singer.
Maybe, but I don't know. But it is pretty. It's a sad pretty pi-
ano song and then a guy singing like he's also sad. But the
guy's not really singing. He's sort of sing-talking. The "Hallelujah" song sounding guy is sing-talking and the words start
with something like: Do you believe in an interventionist
God, do you, don't you?

I'm getting lost a little bit in the music. Meanwhile, Jesus keeps
holding my shoulders steady. The way he's holding my shoulders goes well with the music. I start to realize that my shoulders
have been really tight. Jesus squeezes down on my tight shoulders. I feel my shoulders go a little weak. But not a bad kind of
weak. It's a good kind. Like my shoulders just relaxed for the
first time in a long time.

The music gets louder. It's at the refrain, and the refrain
goes: In my arms of love, hold on. This repeats over and over,
and now I know what song it is. I don't know who sings it, but
I know the song. I know the song. It's "Arms of Love," which
is pretty much the exact right song to come on right now. I
don't know how Jesus got it to play right then, but it's playing. "Arms of Love" by this "Hallelujah" song sounding guy

is playing, and I've got a gun to Jesus's head. I've got a gun to Jesus's head, but my arm is tired from holding the gun to Jesus's head. I put my other hand on my gun hand to help hold the gun up, but it doesn't help. My arm is so tired. My arm and my shoulders and really all of me. I'm just really, really tired now. I want to put the gun down. I want to put the gun down and really all of it. I want to put everything down. But then what? Then what?

Then Jesus moves his hands off my shoulders and on to my face. He's holding my face with both his hands. Cradling my face in his hands. His hands are warm and soft. Warm and soft and strong.

Jesus says: What is it you really want, Reggie? Go ahead. You can tell us. Whatever it is, whatever it is. Whatever it is in your heart of hearts that you most wish for right now?

ASTRONAUTS

Douglas Li is an immigration specialist. His business is to transport undocumented Chinese nationals into the United States. His current consignment consists of twenty-seven beneficiaries from Fujian. Fujian is Douglas's ancestral home. This is just a coincidence. Douglas is not nostalgic. He has no personal motivation to do business in or with Fujian, except that Fujian is a wealthy province. Fujian is a wealthy province, but these beneficiaries are not wealthy. They are coming to the United States to work in a meat factory. They are good at this kind of work. They don't mind the loneliness or the injuries. They don't mind the long, gruesome hours. They don't mind dropping dead, on average, at the age of fifty-two. Fifty-two is just a guess. It could be longer, though Douglas doubts that. They don't mind any of this as long as they get paid, and their money finds its way back to Fujian, to the greedy and/or hungry hands of their gambling-addicted fathers, their crippled brothers, their boyfriends on the down-low, their village leaders, their mothers, their children, their wives.

Until recently, Douglas referred to these kinds of beneficiaries as Coolies. This is an outdated term in the United States.

It was pervasive in the 1800s. It referred to Chinese emigrant workers during the construction of the Transcontinental Railroad and then afterward in immigration and employment legislation. The term literally translates in Mandarin to "Bitter strength." To those who know the term, it is understood as a derogatory description of hard laborers, often who've been indentured or otherwise subjugated. Douglas had used the term both as a practical designation as well as a slur, until he resolved to refer to these laborers simply as Workers. This is not an act of conscience. It is an adoption of what he sees as a more professional aesthetic.

In any case, Douglas does not like them. He does not like working with them. They are not interesting conversationalists. They are not politically influential. They are not rich. Douglas prefers to work with interesting, influential, rich beneficiaries who can pay him to arrange visas and amnesty. He is doing this job under duress, a personal favor to the big boss.

Douglas has had these workers for a week. This is too long. They are in the garage of Granja Roja, a tomato processing facility in the interior of Sinaloa, Mexico. A Mexican man known as Chucho discusses technical parameters with a mechanic. Douglas knows Chucho. They are friendly, but they are not friends. The mechanic slaps his hand onto the wall of a forty-foot shipping container. Chucho frowns and looks up to meet Douglas's eyes. Chucho shakes his head.

The shipping container is used to ship tomatoes. The twenty-seven workers Douglas is transporting will be hidden inside of this container in a stowaway chamber underneath twenty-four specially weighted pallets of tomatoes. It's a complicated set-up, like a magic trick. Everything has to look one way while being another. The sights, the sounds, the weight. It all has to add up to be tomatoes in the observer's eye, but when the magician pulls his hand from the hat, it's workers all the way.

A delivery strategy like this has a hundred ways to go bad. Douglas is not happy about this. If it goes wrong, either they'll get caught and the workers get detained, or the equipment will fail and the workers die. For Douglas, there won't be much difference either way. If the workers get detained or if they die, Douglas will go to prison, if the bosses even let him get to prison.

The bosses want this job done. The last few trucks full of workers have been picked up at the border. Those workers were also hidden inside cargo containers. They were sniffed out by dogs. This cost the bosses money and also respect. The bosses don't want this to happen again. They like Douglas, they say. He's done a good job. But business is business.

Douglas thought to send the workers through the desert on foot. But he realizes he can't send a platoon of Fujianese laborers through the Mexican desert. They'd be killed by the environment almost certainly. Or by bandits, or, on the other side of the border, by vigilantes. Or, stupidly, they could make a run for it, escaping their debt and making a go of America on their own. No, Douglas has no reasonable alternative. The tomato container is the best plan.

Meanwhile, the twenty-seven workers are gathered in a corner of the warehouse. Douglas has literally seen a million of these men in his lifetime, and still he's surprised by how terrible they look: skinny, short, fucked-up teeth, hope-

lessly unkempt hair. Douglas feels like a god next to them.
The workers mostly talk amongst themselves, or sleep. One
seems attentive to Douglas and Douglas's goings on. He nods
at Douglas. Douglas is familiar with this worker. His name is
Yiming. Yiming is young, much younger than Douglas. He
looks youthful enough to be a teenager, but he is probably
at least twenty-five. He smiles a lot. Usually when workers
smile a lot, it means they're embarrassed or scared. But Yiming seems to smile because he's happy. Douglas likes that.

In Mandarin, Yiming says, "*Boss, what's wrong? Can I help?*"

"*I'm not your boss*," says Douglas, not trusting Yiming
to help, but enjoying being called boss. In English, he says,
"There's nothing you can do. Just stay out the way."

Yiming says, "*Thank you, boss. I can help. Your machine.
I've done that work.*"

Douglas ignores him. Yiming taps Douglas on the arm.

Douglas says, "Tsou nee ma. It's fine. Leave it the fuck
alone."

Yiming does not seem bothered. He seems to make an
attempt to comprehend Douglas's English. He mouths *fuck
alone*. Douglas rolls his eyes. Douglas can speak Mandarin
fine, but he enjoys using English with the workers, pretending
it's for their own benefit. He says, "Too bad you aren't a woman. You know what I'm saying? Woman? Piaoliang nuhai?"

Yiming nods with enthusiasm. Douglas pokes a finger to
Yiming's chest, an impolite gesture among Chinese. Yiming
looks down at the finger. Douglas wonders if Yiming will
say anything about it. He says, "You don't like that, huh?"
and scans Yiming's face for anger, but Yiming doesn't seem
bothered.

Douglas says, "Too bad you ain't got money. If only you were some rich Party motherfucker. Yoqian. It's the honey or it's the money. But your ass got neither."

Douglas frowns and turns both his hands over, palms up. He looks at Yiming, who is still smiling. Yiming mimics Douglas's gesture, hands out, palms up. Douglas looks at Yiming, at Yiming's hands, and then at the whole gang of busted-up, broke-ass workers. None of them have much of anything but their hands.

Yiming says, "Wo yo piaoliang nuhai."

Douglas says, "You? Yeah, I don't think so."

Yiming nods. He reaches into his front pants pocket and takes out a wallet. The wallet looks new. It's the size and shape of a checkbook. It has a brass latch securing it. Yiming opens the wallet. There is no money in it, just wallet-sized pictures and other nostalgia. He takes the stack of small pictures out, just three or four, and begins to show them to Douglas. There are two boys in the first two pictures. They look happy, smiling even though most rural Chinese still believe it is bad luck to smile in pictures. He says, "Wo de er zimen."

Douglas laughs, "The fuck you have two sons?" and pats Yiming on the back.

Yiming shows Douglas a third picture. It's of a woman. The woman is wearing a blue dress. She is thick-boned and pale-skinned. She is not smiling, but she has kind eyes. Douglas thinks she has kind eyes.

Douglas says, "Ugly."

Yiming doesn't seem to understand.

Douglas says, "But good. That's a good woman."

He pushes the pictures and the wallet back to Yiming. He

points at Yiming's pocket, "Now put that shit away. Some as-shole's gonna think you have money."

The shipping container ostensibly carries tomatoes. In actu-ality, the twenty-seven workers will be hidden inside of this container. They will be hidden inside a stowaway chamber. The stowaway chamber is designed to be undetectable. Invis-ible, sound-proof, smell-proof. The design of the stowaway chamber is as such: The stowaway chamber is an airtight steel structure contained within a thirty-seven-foot false floor. It is 1.75 feet deep. It runs nearly the entire length of the interior of the container. To avoid detection, the false floor and the stowaway compartment is recessed at least the length of one palette from the gate. This allows at least one row of palettes to be stacked in front of it. The stowaway chamber has a hatch that lifts up and then slides toward the container gate. The hatch is at the back of the trailer. The hatch locks from the inside of the stowaway chamber. This is to minimize its de-tectability. However, it will not be possible to open the hatch while the pallets are still loaded on top of it. The shipping container itself is equipped with an HVAC system. This is separate from the HVAC system mounted inside the stow-away compartment. The stowaway compartment's system is retrofitted with oxygen canisters and a CO_2 filter. This sys-tem is called Life Support.

Chucho yells at his crew in Spanish. Douglas doesn't speak much Spanish, but from the looks of things, there are doubts about Life Support. The apparatus is old, which Chucho ex-plains could be a good thing. It's easier to modify. But the modifications have been elaborate. They've hidden Life Support inside the container in a way that makes it invisible from the outside. But those border customs motherfuckers know every trick. They have likely even seen twenty-seven workers stashed up in a tomato freight before. But border customs is also busy. Border customs is also understaffed. They are also sometimes lazy. So, as long as Douglas doesn't flaunt his operation, it's as likely as not that they won't poke around inside a trailer full of tomatoes. It's like everything in the US and in the whole world, really. Anything is possible. You just need to know the game. You just need to know the loopholes and the shortcuts, the subtext, what's written between the lines, how to skate the edges, how to shoot the gaps. Because, if the illegal thing is indecipherable from the legal, isn't it for all intents and purposes legal?

Douglas walks into the empty container. He stands over the hidden compartment. His thumb is behind his back, hitched into his belt. He has a small revolver tucked in there. He rests the palm of his hand on the gun's hard rubber grips. It is the only firearm on the premises. There is no need for Douglas to carry a firearm. This is for show, an accessory like a tie clip or a handbag or a Rolex watch.

The hidden compartment is underneath the main storage area, where the tomatoes will go. Douglas pats the metal wall of the container. The hidden compartment is typically used to smuggle inanimate things, like drugs or car parts or knockoff toys. Things that don't need Life Support. Douglas stands next to Chucho.

Douglas says, "What's the problem?"

Chucho says, "There's no problem."

"Then what's the holdup?"

"It's the air. Self-contained. Sealed. Dog-proof. But with twenty-seven of these guys packed in there. It's not like you can just turn on the O2 and let it go. Too much and it'll kill 'em. Not enough and it'll kill em."

"You need an engineer."

"We need an engineer."

"We don't have an engineer?"

Chucho doesn't say anything.

Douglas says, "But if you did, and the O2 worked out, then how's the rest?"

Chucho says, "Container's no problem. It's not comfortable. They have to lay down in the dark for eight hours. They crap and piss, they just have to lay in it. But there's no problem. They'll have air."

"What if we get held up?"

"No problem. Once it's set, they can live for days, a week."

Douglas doesn't believe this.

A few feet from the container, some of the workers are gathered around an old tube television set. The television set is not working. Yiming has removed the back of the television and is tinkering with its wiring. Something happens and the television comes on. The other workers applaud. It's the happiest they've been all week.

Yiming comes out from behind the television and takes a seat. He gives the other workers a thumbs up. The other workers laugh at him. The other workers pat him on the back. One worker goes to the television and starts to turn the channel selector knob. He flips through two channels. He stops at an old black-and-white science fiction movie. The audio is turned down low. The worker tries to turn up the volume, but it doesn't get any louder. Yiming leans in close. His head is slightly turned, like he's trying to listen to someone whisper. Douglas walks over to Yiming and pats him on the shoulder.

Douglas says, "*You fixed this.*"

Yiming says, "*Yes, boss.*"

"*No tools?*"

Yiming smiles and shrugs. Douglas nods. He motions for the worker seated next to Yiming to move. The worker moves, and Douglas takes his seat. He then takes out his cigarettes. He offers one to Yiming, who accepts. He lights his own cigarette and passes the lighter to Yiming, who does the same. Yiming holds the cigarettes out to return them to Douglas, but Douglas waves his hand in the air. "You keep those."

Douglas reaches out and turns up the volume knob. It cracks and then gets very loud. Douglas exhales and leans back in the flimsy plastic chair. He pats Yiming on the back and smiles at him. The fuck I care about this little fucking genius, he thinks as he blows smoke into the air. Together they watch the movie. It's near the end. An astronaut is returning to Earth after an eighty-year mission. Upon his arrival, he finds that his lover has not aged. Meanwhile the astronaut has become a very old man. This is not scientifically accurate, but it is how it happens in the movie. The old astronaut then tells his young lover to leave him. She does.

Douglas says, "The fuck was that?"

On the television, a beer commercial comes on. In it, several white people enjoy the beach at sundown. A pit fire is roaring. The music is Spanish guitar. A beautiful woman links arms with a handsome man. They are both young.

Around the television, some of the other workers have

turned their attention to the movie. Their looks vary, from confusion to amusement to sadness. Although they may not be sad. They may be just tired. It's possible that Douglas is projecting his own sadness on to them.

"That show," says Douglas, "is the truth. This is the world, and the joke is on the astronauts. Sacrifice everything. Go across the universe. All for what? You come back worn out, old, and busted up. And nobody cares. Your lover don't care. Your kids don't care. America don't care. Nobody cares."

Yiming says, "*Same as us.*"

Douglas says, "Same as you."

Then Douglas corrects himself, "Same as us."

He grabs Yiming by the back of the neck. He kneads the scruff of the younger man's nape. He feels Yiming relax under his grip. Douglas gestures to the shipping container, "*You fixed this television?*"

"*Yes, boss.*"

"*How?*"

"*I know about electricity. My work.*"

Douglas looks at Yiming. He thinks this is dumb. He thinks there's no way he can trust that some dumbass is gonna fix something even Chucho can't get a handle on. He tells himself to forget about whatever he's thinking about. But still. This guy. Douglas looks at him. This guy is different. There's something in his eyes. Something in his hands. Like a spark or something, an illumination.

Douglas says, "*Can you really fix the truck. The AC?*"

"*Yes, boss,*" says Yiming. "*Yes, I really can.*"

The workers are packed into the hidden compartment. They

are laid down flat on their backs, shoulder to shoulder. They look like sardines in a can. Douglas places Yiming in last, at the far end where the hatch closes.

Douglas says, "First class."

Yiming says, "*Thank you, boss.*"

Douglas pulls the hatch closed. It drops with a clang. The clang echoes inside the empty shipping container. Douglas taps on the hatch. He listens for the sound of the latch securing. He waits. He taps again. Then a dull, clunky click. Douglas stands up and waves to the forklift to load the tomatoes.

Chucho is already sitting behind the wheel inside the tractor trailer cabin. He gives the thumbs up to Douglas. Douglas is silent, listening as the Life Support system hums gently. He turns his head, pressing his right ear to the container. The sound is warm and sustained, like static on the television.

Chucho raps his knuckles on the outside of his door. He looks over to Douglas. "We good?"

Douglas nods back. "We're good."

⟿

Douglas lights a cigarette and smokes without talking. Chucho pulls the truck out of the garage and rumbles onto a hard-packed dirt road. It's just the two of them in the tractor trailer, the two of them and the twenty-seven workers in the cargo. Douglas wanted to have another guy in the cabin for security, but Chucho told him it'd be suspicious. It's already suspicious with a Chinese in the truck. But Douglas has good paperwork. His documents say he's an American citizen, lives in La Habra, California. These are real documents. Douglas is a real American. He's voted in every presidential election since H. W.; Republican every time, except Clinton '96. He even speaks English with a slight southern drawl, which makes no sense except that Douglas likes how it sounds.

The fastest route to New Mexico takes five hours. They're taking a longer route to avoid attention. The early part of the drive follows the western coast of Mexico, close to Mazatlan, facing the Gulf of California. Douglas looks out at the beaches, the layers of blue water. Douglas likes the beach. He plans to retire on the beach. Not Mazatlan. Too many bad memories. It's gotta be someplace he's never been. He doesn't mind the cold. He thinks maybe Seattle. He's never been north of San Francisco.

As the sun is setting, the sky turns orange, and the water turns purple. Douglas closes his eyes. He is tired. He's been on alert for the past week. This is the home stretch. He just has to see the drive through, get the workers to Los Lunas. If everything goes right, they won't even stop at the border. Just get waved through like friends. Good morning. Morning. Morning to you.

Douglas starts to nod off. He tells himself he shouldn't. He should stay awake. It's just another few hours. But the fatigue grabs hold of him. This must be what dying is like. In the end, no drama, just relief. He thinks about Yiming in the cargo. He wonders if it's cold back there. He wonders if Yiming would like to visit him in Seattle. These are his last thoughts before he falls asleep.

Douglas does not sleep well. He wakes up several times. Each time, it's darker than before. It gets to be the kind of dark that is all consuming. Pitch black. He can see the tractor trailer's headlights project beams into the darkness. They illuminate a small spot of road, the asphalt, the markers, and then nothing. No other cars, no road signs, no shadows of the horizon. It's as if the light disintegrates into space, is absorbed by the darkness itself.

Chucho has the stereo on. It's American rock music.

Douglas says, "Que pasa?"

Chucho says, "Nada."

Chucho offers Douglas cocaine. Perico, he calls it. Douglas accepts, taking the vial and preparing a small mound of powder on the fleshy part of his hand. He snorts the cocaine. He licks his forefinger and wipes the residue off his hand, rubbing it into his gums. He drops the vial into his shirt pocket. He makes a mental note to throw the empty vial out the window once he's done. Then he feels the numbness come over his face, seeping in from his nasal cavity and, to a lesser extent, from his mouth. Chucho opens a can of beer and hands it to Douglas. Douglas takes it and sips. He looks out into the darkness. He takes another sip, "How much longer?"

Chucho says, "Que?"

"To the border?"

"Dos horas."

"Bueno, muy bueno."

"So, what?" says Chucho. "You want to fuck that guy?"

"It's not like that," says Douglas. "He's smart. He's too good for this shit."

"So what. If he's so good, he'll move on. He'll do something else. Eventually. Work his way up. Go to college. Get a nice government job. Buy a big house in the oasis. American dream. Right, boss?"

"You know it don't work like that."

"He's not your problem, boss."

"Yeah," says Douglas. "I know."

It's four miles to the border checkpoint. Douglas is wired. He is both drunk and high, his temples are tingling. His eyes aren't blinking. Blink, motherfucker. Blink. The stereo is turned up loud. Douglas turns it up even more. The speakers start to crack. It's still American rock and roll. Douglas shakes his head and slaps his face to clear his thoughts, to get ready to perform for the border agents. A song comes on that Douglas knows. He sings along. He gets the words wrong. He's surprisingly self-conscious. Chucho seems to know the correct words, but he doesn't make a big deal out of it. Douglas appreciates this.

Douglas takes out a travel-sized mouthwash and takes a swig of it. He passes it to Chucho, who does the same. Both men swish the mouthwash around and then gargle. Douglas spits his out the window. Chucho follows suit. Douglas then fishes the empty cocaine vial out of his pocket and tosses it out the window as well. He does the same with the beer cans, one after another. As they go, some of them catch the wind and whap against the side of the cargo container.

The song they were singing along to ends. Douglas sees something from his side mirror. Headlights. The headlights are closing in on them. "Fuck is that?"

Chucho turns his head to look out the rearview mirror. Douglas sticks his head out the window a little bit and turns to look out back. A bright spotlight turns on and shines into his eyes.

Chucho says, "Federales."

A federal police pickup truck is behind them. It flashes its lightbar, red and blue and white. The brightness cuts through the dark. Douglas squints and bangs a fist on the dashboard.

"It's fine," says Chucho. "Stay cool, boss."

Chucho points to the cargo and makes a shush gesture. Douglas quiets down. He listens. The noise has stopped. Behind them, the police instruct them in Spanish and then English to pull over. Chucho downshifts the tractor trailer, going backwards through the gears. They slow and come to a stop on the dirt shoulder. Then the police pickup pulls in front of them.

Chucho says, "I'll deal with this."

Chucho holds his hand out to Douglas. Douglas hands Chucho a small roll of hundred-dollar bills. Chucho looks disappointed, but Douglas doesn't give him any more. Chucho puts the money in his pocket just as one officer comes to his window. Another officer stands underneath Douglas's window. This one is holding a shotgun.

In Spanish, the first officer says, "*What's in the cargo?*"

Chucho says, "Tomates."

"*Tomatoes? Really? That's an extravagant transport for tomatoes.*"

"*They're special. Artisanal.*"

"*What?*"

"*Special*," says Chucho. "*They are special tomatoes.*"

The officer with the shotgun starts to walk over to the cargo container. He taps the shotgun against the container wall.

The second officer says, "Jefe, *there's something strange about this cargo.*"

The officer with the shotgun waits for a response. Douglas smiles at him and tries to act as if he is slightly bored by the process. He eyes the container through his mirror. He listens. The hum of the machinery rumbles on, but the workers stay quiet. It's soundproof, he tells himself. It's soundproof. But Douglas hears something. He thinks he hears something. A voice. A knock. A breath. Breathing. Breathing. Then nothing.

Douglas reaches behind his back, feeling the handle of his revolver. He feels a coldness. The coldness starts in his arms and moves into his middle. Douglas has only rarely fired his gun, and never at a living thing. Chucho puts a hand on Douglas's elbow. Douglas looks at Chucho. Chucho shakes his head.

The officer under Chucho's window says, "*You think we need to see your tomatoes?*"

This is an invitation for a bribe.

Chucho says, "*You're welcome to. But why waste time?*"

The officer says, "*True. It's been a long night. My partner has been itching to get home to his new wife.*"

Chucho laughs. The officer under Chucho's window laughs. The officer with the shotgun underneath Douglas's window does not laugh. It's not clear if he hasn't heard the conversation or if he disapproves of them joking about his wife.

The officer under Chucho's window gestures for Chucho to get out of the cabin. Chucho opens his door. It swings heavy and then clicks open. Chucho steps out. Douglas waits. The officer with the shotgun keeps a flashlight pointed at Douglas. Douglas tries not to let this annoy him, but it is annoying. He squints and tries to look the officer in the face. He knows this is dumb. The officer isn't going to want to be seen by Douglas,

to be recognizable by him. But Douglas is drawn to the illumination, the other man's face framed by the police truck's
spotlights like a halo. I don't know this man, thinks Douglas.
He could kill me. He could help me. And I don't know him.
And I never will.

~

They get to the border. The American border guards do not
detain the tractor trailer. Douglas talks to a customs officer,
who is looking over their paperwork. The customs officer
says, "California, huh? So how 'bout them Dodgers?"

"Shit," says Douglas. "K.B.'s a boss, am I right?"

"Yeah, right," says the customs officer. "More like a choke
artist."

Douglas laughs. The officer waves at Chucho to get rolling.

Chucho keeps his eyes straight ahead. He drives the tractor
trailer off the scales and through the inspection corridor and
back onto the highway.

From the cargo comes the steady whirl and hum of the
HVAC equipment. They drive for the next two hours. Douglas is anxious. Douglas's head hurts. Douglas does not feel
sleepy again. He tells himself not to worry. He tells himself
it's the cocaine. He sits and watches as the sun rises to his
right. Long, orange rays stretch across the desert sky and
backlights the shadows of the jagged shiprock. As he watches,
Douglas thinks he'll have a cup of hot coffee when he gets to
Los Lunas. He'll read the morning paper, and maybe there'll
be a dog there. He'll pet the dog. He'll pour an extra cup for
Yiming, and the two will sit and chat about world events, a

friendly argument over the sovereignty of Taiwan. He rolls his window down. The cold comes in. He holds his hands to his mouth and breathes into them, warming them.

When they arrive in Los Lunas, there's no one there to greet them. Douglas gets out of the cabin and unlocks the gates. He stays out of the tractor trailer and waves to Chucho to drive in. Chucho pulls the truck through the gates and forward past the cargo bay. He backs the truck into a delivery door. Douglas stands up on the bay. He doesn't bother to guide Chucho. Chucho doesn't seem to need it.

Douglas opens the container. Chucho uses a forklift to take the tomato pallets out. He does this one pallet out at a time. Each pallet has fifteen rows of packaged tomatoes stacked on top of it. The tomatoes look perfect. They are red and round. They look like they'd be delicious to bite into.

Douglas watches as Chucho works to unload the pallets. Chucho takes each into the storage area. He arranges them against a wall. As he watches Chucho, the anxious feeling continues to bother Douglas. The container is too quiet. He tells himself it's supposed to be quiet. That's the whole point. But wouldn't there be some noise, something? Knocking, shouting, something? But except for the HVAC, there is nothing. Douglas bangs his fist on the side of the forklift. "Hurry it up. We gotta get this shit open."

Chucho says, "Something wrong, boss?"

"Yeah. Just hurry the fuck up. Come on."

Chucho works faster. He unloads the pallets without arranging them. Douglas goes into the shipping container. The hatch is slightly ajar. Douglas grabs at its edge but he can't open it. It's still blocked. Douglas shouts through the hatch opening, "You guys okay? Yiming? You okay?"

There is no response. Chucho gets the last obstructing pallet out. It's still quiet. Douglas grabs the hatch edge. It catches against the recessed opening. Chucho jumps off the forklift and comes beside Douglas. Together they drag the hatch up and away. They drop the hatch. It lands crooked, half in the container and half out. Underneath, the workers are motionless, piled as if they were tossed about like dolls in a toy chest. The workers look blue, mostly eyes closed, some eyes open and bloodshot. Many of them have their arms positioned over their chests, their hands clasped over their hearts.

Chucho says, "Dang, boss. This is bad."

In the pile, Douglas sees Yiming. Yiming looks worse than the others. He is pale blue like them, but he is also mangled. His face is beaten, his eyes swollen shut, blood streaked across from his mouth and nose, from his ears even.

Douglas says, "Fucking shit, Yiming."

Yiming lays still. Douglas squats down next to him. He reaches in and touches Yiming's hand. Yiming's hand moves slightly. His hand opens a bit and closes a bit. Douglas grabs hold of the hand, "Goddamn it. He's not dead. Help me get him out."

Chucho says, "No, fuck this guy. Fuck him. This is on him. He was supposed to fix that shit. This is on him, boss."

Douglas says, "It's not his fault."

"Don't be stupid," says Chucho. "Don't make this worse than it already is."

Douglas ignores Chucho. He holds on to Yiming's hand and pulls. Yiming groans. He's alive, but barely. Douglas looks into Yiming's broken face. Yiming whispers, "Wo yao hui jia. Wo yao hui jia. Bang mang wo. Bang mang. *I want to go home. I want to go home. Help me. Help.*"

~

A week since Los Lunas, and Chucho is gone. Douglas paid him to lay low and keep his mouth shut. Chucho probably won't keep his mouth shut, at least not for very long. Douglas is in Las Vegas. He's there to meet one of the bosses. Yiming is not with Douglas. Yiming is in a motel in Henderson. He's there alone. He's still a mess. But he's not as big of a mess as he was a week ago. His face is fucked up. His arm is broken and will probably never really be set right. He can't see out one eye. But he is alive.

The boss that Douglas is meeting is the middle boss. Not the big boss, but not the little boss either. When he heard that the middle boss was coming, Douglas didn't think that was a good sign. He thought that probably meant he had an 80–20 chance of leaving Las Vegas alive. That's 20 percent alive, 80 percent not. Douglas gets to the bar and sees the middle boss seated in a booth. It's not a good thing that the boss had to wait for Douglas. Douglas tries to recalculate his odds of survival. Before he can come up with a number, a waitress stops him and asks if he's there to meet the boss. Douglas nods.

The bar is opulent. The ceilings are gold. The walls are gold. The chairs are plush white leather, soft and clean. The waitress is Chinese American. She has long blonde hair and wears a short skirt. As she gets to the boss's table, the boss asks her advice about which sports car he should buy next. The waitress says Corvette. The boss says he already has a Corvette, it's a piece of shit. The waitress laughs.

Douglas doesn't talk to the waitress. He watches the casino. There are a lot of Chinese there. The waitress leaves. The boss doesn't look at Douglas.

The boss says, "You should do something else."

Douglas says, "Yeah."

"What, is this the mafia? You in for life? Get a government job, like the post office."

"No thanks."

"What, you're too good for the post office?"

Douglas is not too good for the post office. He'd probably like working at the post office. He wishes he maybe had taken a post office job instead of this one.

Douglas says, "Yeah, I'm too good for the post office."

Douglas takes out his mobile phone. He doesn't have any new messages. He scrolls through the old ones. The boss watches as Douglas does this. Douglas knows it's bad form. The boss doesn't say anything, which is worse than if he did. Douglas puts the phone down.

Douglas says, "You're here to find out what happened?"

The boss says, "I already know what happened."

Douglas continues, "It was genius. We had them in this refrigerated tomato freight. It was genius, greased and smell-proof, dog-proof. We had all the lackeys bribed, and that state-of-the-art Life Support keeping fresh air pumped in the whole time. We thought we could leave them workers in that box for a week if we had to. Even with the piss and shit, it'd stink, but as long as that Life Support worked, nobody was gonna die."

The boss motions for Douglas to go ahead and try to explain.

Douglas goes on, "But the Life Support didn't work. It makes noise like it's working, but something's not working. Those workers in the freight, but the air, it starts to run out. These fuckers can't breathe right. It gets bad. Some of them pass out early. Some probably died early, the older ones, maybe. The fat ones, not that there were any fat ones. Then there's this one guy. The one guy I knew, Yiming. This guy. My guy. This fucking guy is closest to the hatch. He was trying to get it open. The other workers pushed at him. But it was my guy, trying to open the hatch. But the other workers are crushing him. He couldn't get enough space to turn the handle. It's this long ass naval latch. The door won't open. Of course, it won't open. Goddamn who knows how many tons of tomatoes on top of it. These workers, they get desperate. The ones that have any strength in them start to grab at my guy. Grab him, yanking his arms, his head, his legs. They start to hit and kick. Cursing him. But he's just trying to help. They punch and elbow and grab and pull, tearing at his eyeballs and his jaw. Fucking him up to kingdom come, using up even more air while they're at it.

"By the time me and Chucho get the box opened, they're goners. Just a pile of cold, dead corpses. Except then, like a zombie movie, there's something in there. Something moving. This hand, this one hand reaches out. Chucho says to leave it. But I'm a dumbass good Samaritan. I grab that hand and pull it forward, but the arm is limp like a rope. I pull it forward, and this guy comes out. And it's my guy, Yiming. I pull him out, sort of out. It's just his arm and shoulder and head out. He's got blood coming out his eyes and ears and black puke coming out his mouth. His face is all punched in, nose practically torn off, eyes swollen shut. And he's trying to say something, in fucking Foochow, he's saying something. But I can't hear him. I lean in. I can still barely hear him. It just sounds like a slow stutter. Like tiny puffs of air coming out one puff at a time. I tell him, What? What is it? He reaches his hand out for me, and he's saying, help, help, help."

Douglas takes out another couple cigarettes and gives the boss one. He lights his own and then, with the same match, lights the boss's. They inhale, almost in unison, and then blow smoke out the sides of their mouths. The boss waits for Douglas to finish the story, but Douglas doesn't say anything more.

The boss says, "So, what did you do then?"

Douglas puts his cigarette in his mouth and leaves it there. The cigarette twitches a tiny bit, each time he pulls. Looking at the boss, he leans back and hitches his thumbs into his belt.

"What'd I do?" says Douglas. "I helped him."

"What do you mean you helped him?"

He keeps his eyes on the boss's eyes. Douglas makes a gun gesture with his thumb and forefinger. He points his forefinger at his temple, a pretend gun like he's about to blow his own brains out. Then Douglas makes a clicking sound with his tongue. He moves his thumb like how a gun's hammer would hit its firing pin. He juts his head to the side. He does these gestures methodically.

The boss frowns and finishes his drink, "Jesus, you didn't have to do that."

Douglas doesn't say anything.

"Well, could have been worse," the boss says. "You wouldn't

believe some of these dumbshits. They have a come to Jesus. They think they're gonna help these fuckers. Sneak them out. Set them free."

Douglas says, "Dumbshits."

The boss says, "That shit doesn't end well."

"Nope," says Douglas. "Not for nobody."

The boss makes a face. The face is a half-frown and half-smile. He shakes his head at Douglas.

The boss says, "You're no dumbshit though. Hard ass."

Douglas says, "Rock hard," and raps his knuckles on the table top.

The boss doesn't say anything else. Douglas can't tell if the boss believes his story. Douglas can't tell if it matters. The waitress comes over to retrieve the boss's empty glass. She holds the tab out to the boss. The boss smiles and points at Douglas. "It's on him."

The waitress puts the tab down on the table without looking at Douglas. She then puts her hand on the boss's arm. The boss gets up, and the two of them walk toward the casino. Douglas stays seated. He watches. The boss doesn't look back. The boss gives the waitress something else, his number maybe, maybe his room card. The waitress kisses the boss on the cheek. The boss leaves the casino.

Douglas looks around. He sees some guys. These guys might be the boss's guys. They might be waiting for Douglas to leave. They might be getting ready to grab him and drive him out to the desert and beat him up some and then bury him under a rock. Or not. They might be just regular Vegas Chinese. They might just be regular Chinese guys looking to gamble and maybe get laid. Douglas doesn't know. He doesn't know what will happen now. But he thinks his odds are still bad. His odds are still just as bad as ever.

He picks up his drink. He finishes it slowly, letting the last drops of liquid drain into his mouth, and then a piece of ice. He clanks the piece of ice around in his mouth and then spits it back into the glass and then places the glass onto the table-top, before picking up the bill and looking it over.

Douglas takes out a wallet. It's the size and shape of a checkbook. It has a brass latch securing it. It's Yiming's wallet.

Douglas opens the latch. He takes out a small stack of bills. Several small pictures fall out as he does this. Douglas takes the pictures and spreads them out on the table. He arranges them in rows. The pictures include the one of Yiming's sons. There is also the one of Yiming's wife, and then other pic-tures that Douglas hasn't seen yet, a picture of a hilly field, a picture of the side of a house, an old car that doesn't look to run. Finally, there is a picture of a man, who might be Yim-ing. The man is carrying a bicycle on his shoulder as he walks up a set of stairs. A young boy walks beside the man. The picture is taken from behind them, so you cannot see their faces. The picture is in black and white. The man carrying the bicycle is holding the young boy's hand. They are almost to the top of the stairs. The stairs seem to lead to a doorway. The doorway seems to lead out into the outdoors. The outdoors is overexposed, just a white light that bleeds into the stairway and surrounds the man and the boy, washing them in a glow like supernatural beings, like ghosts, or just normal people caught in a twilight, in-between where they're coming from and where they are going.

THE DONKEY IS DEFINITELY ASIAN

I sit with Marvin in front of my childhood elementary school.
Marvin is my grandfather. He's in his wheelchair. I'm on a
park bench. Marvin snaps his fingers.

He says: Come on, Reggie.

I say: No.

He says: Cigarette.

I shake my head and take out two cigarettes. I light them
together and hand one to him.

I say: I don't want to get blamed for this.

He says: What do you care?

He takes a long drag and holds his breath for a second, and
then blows out a big cloud of smoke. He scoffs and points to
the playground. The playground equipment is in the shape of
animals. He points out the donkey.

He says: That one was your favorite.

I say: That was a long time ago.

He says: Donkey's not a lucky animal for Chinese people.

I say: I don't believe in luck.

He says: Well, not always unlucky. Depends how you see it.

We smoke without talking for a couple seconds, maybe a

minute. I take short drags and try to make smoke rings. Then Marvin starts telling me about this story.

He says: Remember that story about the magic donkey?

I say: Kinda.

He says: You liked that story.

I say: I don't really remember.

He finishes his cigarette and flicks it on to the grass. He asks for another one. I put my cigarette out on the armrest of the bench. Then I get up and snuff out Marvin's with my shoe. I pick up both butts and look for a trashcan. There's no trashcan. I put the butts in my pocket. Then I light two new cigarettes and give one to Marvin. He takes his without thanking me. He then starts telling me the donkey story. I tell him stop. He either doesn't hear or doesn't care. He keeps going. I lean back and smoke and look up through the trees and the sky. There's sunshine and shadows and the fluffy kind of clouds. Marvin tells the story. It's a story about a magic donkey. The story goes like this:

Every day, the wise man takes a long walk along the kingdom's border. He needs to do this every day or else the kingdom will collapse. But one day the wise man trips over a tree root and breaks his ankle. He knows that he won't be able to finish that day's long walk. He sits down and thinks about the collapse of the kingdom.

Then, the donkey appears.

The donkey asks the wise man, what's up?

The wise man explains the situation.

The donkey says: I can help. You can ride me.

The wise man accepts, and the donkey carries him and together they finish the long walk.

When they finish, the wise man's kingdom does not collapse and so he's happy and thankful. But he's also worried. He's worried because he knows that he won't be able to do the long walk tomorrow because of his broken ankle.

The donkey says: What's the matter?

The wise man explains.

The donkey says: Yeah, that's a problem.

Then, the wise man gets this idea. He gets this idea to keep the donkey around so as to make the long walk easier.

The wise man says: Stay with me. I'll take care of you. I'll feed you and house you. I'll love you as if you were my own child.

The donkey says: Thank you for the offer, but I think I have to get going.

The donkey starts to leave, but the wise man puts a magic spell on the donkey. The spell turns the donkey into a piece of paper. The wise man walks up to the donkey, who is now a piece of paper. He picks up the paper donkey into his hands and folds it in half. And he folds it again. And then again. He folds the paper donkey up until it is the size of a small envelope. He then puts it in his pocket for the night.

The next day, the wise man takes the paper donkey out from his pocket and unfolds it and it turns back into a regular donkey.

The two stare at each other for a minute. The donkey looks mad but also scared.

The wise man says: Don't be mad.

He gives the donkey a carrot.

The wise man says: Don't be scared.

He gives the donkey an apple.

Then the wise man climbs onto the donkey's back and rides it again and together they do the long walk. And the next day, they do it again. And then the next day, again. And again. And so on. All the while, the kingdom does not collapse.

Marvin slows down toward the end of telling the story. He nods his head like he's thinking something very serious. He nods at me like he's expecting for me to say something. I don't say anything. He asks me if I know what the donkey's magic is. I don't know what the donkey's magic is.

I say: It talks.

He says: Come on, Reggie.

I say: I don't know. It folds up.

He says: You really don't know?

I say: Give me a clue.

He says: The donkey's magic is that it never refuses to serve.

I say: That's not magic.

He says: The donkey is definitely Asian.

I say: What does that mean?

He says: You know, Asians always suffer in silence.

I look at Marvin.

I say: That's some stupid shit, Marvin.

He says: I don't mean anything. It's a joke.

I say: It's not funny.

He says: It's funnier in Chinese.

I say: I doubt that.

We sit. We smoke in silence. We watch the school yard.

There isn't much going on. The kids come out for recess. Marvin waves at them. We finish our cigarettes. I light two more.

He says: Gan xie.

I say: Don't thank me.

He says: I'm fine. I don't have lung cancer.

I'm about to say that it still can't be good for him, when Marvin's breathing starts to tighten up. He wheezes. His eyes clench.

I say: Marvin? Don't fuck around.

Marvin doesn't answer. He closes his eyes. I yell for help. I shake him. I slap at his back. I say his name. I call out again. A woman runs up from the school. A man behind her shouts that she is a doctor. The woman runs fast. She takes me by the arm and moves me aside. She tells me to call 911. She takes Marvin from his wheelchair and puts him on the ground. She checks his heart. She checks his breath.

They won't let me ride with Marvin. Instead I ride in the fire truck. It seems weird. They put earmuffs on my head. I feel like a little kid. I feel like this is supposed to be fun, like a field trip.

Marvin had lost consciousness. The last thing he said to me was: I don't have lung cancer. I wonder if those will be the last words he'll ever say to me. They get him to the hospital. They keep him alive. They say he doesn't have much time though. They say I should tell people. I try to think of who to tell. It takes me a while to think of who I'm going to tell.

The next day and then the next couple days, things move strangely. I would have thought it'd be a blur. I'd have thought it'd be fast and hectic. But in reality, it's slow. It's a lot of sitting around. It's boring, but also busy and also scary. I think, this must be what war is like. Then I think, no, not war. Not war, but something like it.

Thinking of war makes me think of death and thinking of death makes me think to call Marvin's old-folks' home. I call, and a lot of the people from the home come by to see him. A bunch of the old guys come by and also a couple of the helpers and a couple of the nurses. The old guys cry a lot. I wasn't expecting that. I had thought old people would be used to this kind thing.

After that, I think to call Ed. Ed is my dad. Marvin is Ed's dad, so I figure Ed should know. I leave a message. I tell him where we are and that Marvin's probably going to be dead soon. Two days later, Ed shows up. I hadn't seen him since I was little. Coincidentally, the last time I remember seeing him was also in a hospital. That time it was my mom.

When Ed walks into Marvin's room, I'm alone and watching a YouTube about tightrope walking. Marvin's in the OR, some last-ditch thing with his intestines. Ed walks in and doesn't say anything, so I don't see him at first. When I do see him, he smiles at me. I try to smile back, but it feels weird, so I stop.

Ed says: Well, Reggie. You lost weight.

I say: What's up, Ed.

I look at him for what seems like a long time. He looks old. He looks like he could be Marvin's brother instead of his son. But he is tall. And he's lean and he looks strong. He wears his hair long. It's layered and brushed back. He looks a lot like an old Asian Kurt Russell. That's the next thing I say to him.

I say: You look like Asian Kurt Russell.

Ed laughs.

Ed says: Your mom used to say that.

I tell Ed that Marvin's been sick for a while. He says that he knows. We sit around in the room for a while. He watches the rest of the video with me, and then we eat together in the cafeteria, and then we walk around town and then sit around again. And then we walk back to the hospital. It's like we're in the music montage part of a movie. It's stupid, but it's okay.

When we get back to the hospital, Ed stops at the parking lot. I take out my cigarettes. I light one. I offer the pack to him. He declines.

Ed says: I'm not going back in.

I say: Yeah. Okay.

We stand for second, and then I turn to go back inside. Ed puts his hand on my elbow.

Ed says: Hold up.

I stop and turn back around.

I say: What's up?

Ed shrugs.

Ed says: I don't know. Feel like I should say something.

I say: Yeah, well, you don't have to.

Ed says: Yeah. I really don't know what to say.

I say: Okay.

Ed says: The thing is. I thought Marvin would be better for you. You know that.

I say: It's fine.

Ed says: Yeah. You know when I knew?

I say: We don't need to talk about it.

Ed says: It was when you started at that school. Your mom had just died. And me and Marvin were taking you to school.

But you didn't want to go. I can still remember. You were screaming. Screaming crazy like an animal. You screamed so loud. Daddy. No. Daddy. Don't leave me here. Daddy. Don't leave me.

Ed stops. He takes a breath.

I say: I don't remember that.

Ed says: I don't know why, but that shit bothered me so bad. In my guts and all over my skin.

My cigarette had burned to the filter. I flick at the ember. It comes off and tumbles on to the ground. I toss the butt into a trashcan. Ed looks at me. He looks like he's mad now.

Ed says: You mad?

I say: No.

Ed says: Why you mad?

I say: I'm not mad.

Ed says: You think I'm the bad guy.

I say: I never said that.

Ed says: And what, Marvin's the good guy, right.

I say: I didn't say that.

Ed says: You think Marvin's the good guy, but you don't know what he was like. What he used to be like. How mean he was. How scary he was. You don't know.

I don't say anything. I just shake my head and look at him.

Ed says: You don't know.

I say: You don't know either.

Ed looks at me. He still looks mad, but also sad and maybe surprised. He looks sad and maybe surprised and he's quiet for a couple seconds. I think he's thinking of what to say. I think he's trying to apologize. I'm pretty sure he's going to apologize. But then he doesn't. He just looks at me for a long time. I look at him too. I look at his face. He doesn't look like the bad guy. He looks nice. I'm not expecting that. But that's how he looks. It's in his eyes. The niceness. Then he waves his hands around and says: It was good to do this.

I say: Yeah.

Ed says: I mean it.

I say: Yeah. Same here.

Then Ed says to me: You keep it real now.

I say: You know it.

Then he's quiet. I'm quiet too. I light another cigarette. Ed motions at me for one. I give him the pack and the lighter. He lights a cigarette. We both smoke. We smoke without talking for five, six minutes, until we're both done. At almost the same time, we flick our cigarettes to the ground and grind them out with our shoes. A car pulls up. Sports car. Camaro. There's a young Chinese guy driving. The Chinese guy waves at me. Ed nods and doesn't introduce the guy. Ed then gets into the car, and that's the end of that.

About a week later, Marvin and I are alone in the morning. The past couple days he's been coming in and out of consciousness. Sometimes he wakes up and he's normal and joking around. Other times he's calling me Ed. I tell him Ed had stopped by but then had to get going. Then once I just pretend that I am Ed and that seems actually kind of nice for Marvin and for me too. Then he's out again, and then he's up and normal again, and then later he's back to being confused.

But that morning, he's quiet. He seems to be at peace. I think maybe he's getting better. I pull open the curtains. We're facing west, so we can't see the sun rise. But we can see light falling on the horizon. We can see the shadows from the hospital. I stand there for a minute and watch. I can almost see the ocean.

Then I turn around, and Marvin's face is all bent up. I ask him if he's okay. Then Marvin springs up and grabs holda me. This startles the shit out of me, but I try not to resist. I hold him as best as I can. I try not to press on him. He says something in Chinese, but I don't know what he's saying.

He says: Yuyan! Ni zai na!

I say: I'm here, Ahgong. I'm here.

He looks at me like he doesn't know who I am. Then he seems like he does know who I am. Then he asks me about Taiwan.

He says: We need to go back.

I say: What?

He says: Taiwan.

I have never been to Taiwan.

He says: We have to hurry.

I say: It's okay, Marvin.

He says: You're okay?

I say: I'm okay.

He says: I was scared.

I say: We're okay.

He says: I'm afraid.

I nod.

He breathes heavy. He looks like he's looking at me, but his eyes are glossed over so it's hard to know.

He says: I don't know what to do.

I nod.

I want to take Marvin by the shoulders. I want to shake

him and say something in Chinese. I can't speak Chinese, but if I could, I'd say: Ahgong, wo mingbai.

I'd say: Ahgong, Wo zai zhe. Wo zai zhe. Wo bu hui likai.

But I don't know how to say those things, so I don't say those things. I don't take him by the shoulders. I don't shake him. I don't say those things. I just sit and watch.

Marvin quiets down. He inhales deep. He inhales deep as he can. He takes my hand. He takes my hand into both of his. His palms feel cold and dry and still strong. He holds on tight, pressing my hand, flattening it, folding it.

THERE ARE NO MORE SECRETS
ON PLANET EARTH

Bella Chiang and her father, Reggie, are sitting on his couch. They're in Reggie's living room in front of his new Ectoscope™ Screen. Reggie is having trouble with the technology. A scam is going around where scammers are promising that they can erase timelines from Ectoscope™ for a fee. This fee is substantial. Reggie has paid this fee.

The problem is that nothing can be erased from Ectoscope™. That would be like trying to erase the Universe itself. You can't erase the Universe. And ultimately that's what Ectoscope™ is, literally, The Universe Itself.

Someone with superior technological skills or financial assets might be able to temporarily block or black out sections of the visible Ectoscope™ timeline, but these are just stopgap solutions. Even if the Ectoscope™ timeline could be altered, the technology behind Ectoscope™ has reached critical mass. Soon Ectoscope™ will be just one retailer out of many for timeline observation. Even Google and Facebook, the dinosaurs of the technology industry, have developed new and improved scopes and will enter the timeline market within the year. There's nothing anyone can do to stop this. There are no more secrets on planet Earth. That's just a reality that people will have to get used to.

Every secret ever lied about, covered up, buried, or repressed is now available for all to see, or is in the process of becoming available for all to see. The entire history of Earth, viewable by anyone with a $10,000/week subscription to Ectoscope™ or even a pocket full of credits to pump into a pay-by-the-minute Ectoscope™ Arcade machine.

Who would've thought time travel would turn out like this. No complicated machines, no wormholes, no lightning orbs, no silver DeLoreans, no spaceships slingshotting around the sun, no ancient magic awoken from the tomb of Qin Shi Huang.

None of that.

Just a really powerful telescope. A telescope with unlimited resolution and computers to track the trajectory of Earth's reflection through space from today all the way back to the Big Bang.

Reggie says, "But there are still a lot of things that we can't see. Why can't we just make my history a part of that?"

Bella says, "A part of what, dad?"

"A part of that timeline that we still can't see!"

Reggie is agitated. Bella knows this tone of voice. Reggie is frustrated over not being able to communicate. He's frustrated over not understanding how things are now or how things work. The world has become strange to him. He doesn't like it.

Bella says, "Dad, I told you, it's not like that. It's not that people are erasing parts of the timeline, it's just that the timeline isn't fully rendered yet."

"What do you mean? I just want my life to stay like it is. I don't want anyone to see my life, Isabelle. I don't want that!"

"Oh, Dad, come on."

Bella is frustrated now.

"Look," she says, "we're all in the same boat. Everybody has things in their past that they're embarrassed about. But this is how things are now. No more secrets."

"No, Isabelle, no."

He shakes his head and grabs hold of Bella's shirt collar.

"Please, sweetheart. Help me."

Bella carefully and gently loosens his grip and takes his hands off her collar. She then places his hands into his lap and pats them.

"Dad, remember how people used to be embarrassed about their bodies?"

She emphasizes the word: people.

"Remember how people didn't want other people to see them naked? And first it was just hackers and creepy photographers, and then Periscope™ came out, and then Scan-X™, and then Mimico™?"

"That's not the same thing."

"Yes, Dad. It is. It's exactly the same thing. People used to think they couldn't live if everyone saw them naked. That they'd be so ashamed. And then, one day, everybody could see everybody else naked, and it was no big deal. It actually all worked out fine."

Reggie reaches out and grabs at Bella's shirt collar again. He is clutching too tightly now to be removed without force.

"Fine for who?"

Reggie is referring to the suicides that followed the mass

marketing of Mimico™, which wasn't even actual pictures of naked people, just a computer model of what someone most likely looks like naked. Bella puts her hands on Reggie's wrists. She can feel the scarring on the undersides. She frowns, unable to hide her judgment.

"You can't do this, Dad. Not again. I can't do this again. Please, for me. Be reasonable. Do not freak out."

She looks at Reggie. Reggie's eyes are full of tears, but it seems like he's trying very hard to not break down. Bella takes her hands away and starts to access the Ectoscope™. She calls up Ancient History.

"Let's watch something," say says, "okay? To take our minds off of this. Give us some perspective."

Bella pulls up Jesus of Nazareth, a favorite of hers.

"See, Dad. If Jesus can handle this, so can we. Right?"

The Jesus story (as with many of the major religions) has turned out to be surprisingly accurate to conventional religious belief. It turns out Jesus really was born in a manger. Jesus really did walk on water. Jesus really did turn water into wine. Jesus really was crucified. Jesus really did return from the dead. Jesus really did then fly up into Heaven. It turns out all of that actually happened.

But that was just a few days out of his life. People were curious about what else Jesus did. And it turns out that Jesus was a busy man. Besides the public speaking gigs, which took up just a few hours a week, Jesus mostly liked to party. He and his friends got drunk most days, like crazy stupid drunk, which was unusual in that time and place. He also had a habit of getting into fistfights (he was surprisingly bad at fighting, given that he had supernatural powers at his disposal. It's speculated that he purposefully restrained himself so as to make the fights fair). And then there was Bella's favorite discovery. It turns out that that Jesus was a solid gold-star sex machine with the ladies and the gents.

Traditional religious people did not like this. But something happened. Most everybody else really liked *this* Jesus. They liked him a lot. They liked that he was a lush, and that he got his ass kicked on a regular basis. They loved that he was a maestro in the bedroom (The Jesus *I'm a Lover Not a Fighter* T-shirt became the most popular fashion statement of 2037). Christianity had its biggest popularity explosion since the Nicene Council.

Bella tunes the Jesus timeline feed to the scene of Jesus washing Simon Peter's feet.

She and Reggie watch attentively.

Jesus is smiling as he washes, like he's really enjoying himself. His hands, which are rather large and meaty, rub and knead the feet of his disciple, Simon Peter. Simon Peter seems embarrassed.

There's no audio, but Bella imagines Jesus telling Simon Peter: Hey, don't be embarrassed, man. We're just humans being humans. Whatever it is you're feeling, whatever it is that's bothering you, it's gonna be okay.

And then, and this is Bella's favorite part, Simon Peter shoves Jesus away and draws his sword. He yells something. Jesus puts his arms out, and Simon Peter takes a swing at him. The sword passes through Jesus as if he were a ghost. Simon Peter drops the sword and falls to his knees. Jesus picks him up and holds him. The two men weep.

Bella and Reggie say, in near unison, "Oh, God, that's beautiful."

They look at each other and laugh. Reggie pinches Bella's cheek. Bella lets him, even though she's annoyed by it.

Bella says, "Dad?"

Reggie says, "Yes, Isabelle?"

"What is it that you're so afraid of people seeing?"

Bella tries to imagine what it could be. She thinks about their lives together, all the things they've been through. They've been through some bad times. Reggie and Bella's mother fought, a lot, and bad. Could Reggie have done something awful to her mom? Beat her? Cheated on her? And then Bella's mother died in a car accident, and then Reggie changed. He wasn't angry anymore, but also never really happy either. Maybe there's something there. Maybe Reggie killed Mom? No, that's crazy. Or is it? Or maybe it was something even further back, something in Reggie's past before Bella was even born, some crime that was long buried but never forgotten. Reggie never talked about his life from before Bella was born. Maybe it was some kind of criminal stuff. Or some sex stuff. Jesus, Bella thinks. She's okay with sex stuff, mostly. But there are exceptions. She doesn't really want to think about what those exceptions are.

Reggie says, "I'm sorry, Isabelle. I am."

"What?" she says. "It doesn't have anything to do with me, does it?"

Reggie looks away. Bella looks up. She watches as he suffers, the tension in his jaw, the discomfort in his eyes. Reggie breathes unevenly and too quickly, as if starting to hyperventilate and then panic. Bella scoots over and puts her arm around him.

Reggie says, "Oh, Isabelle. I'm so sorry."

Bella says, "Ah shit, Dad. It's okay. Whatever it is. It's okay."

Reggie scoots away from her, pulling out from under her arm. He raises his head. He is frowning.

"I don't know how to say this."

"Just say it, Dad."

"Bella," he says, and then pauses again.

"Jesus, Dad!"

"Okay, okay!" he says. "Bella, I am not your dad."

The statement confuses Bella. She freezes for a second and then flinches visibly.

"What?"

"Oh, damn it, Isabelle. I'm sorry. It's all a mess. But I'm not your dad. I'm not your father. I don't know who your father is. But it isn't me. I couldn't have kids. Your mother didn't know. But I knew. I couldn't. And when she got pregnant with you, I confronted her. She swore you were mine. But then the tests came back, and they said there was no chance you were mine. I was so mad, honey. I went crazy. I tracked down every guy your mother was close to. Her ex-boyfriends. Her coworkers. Even her church pastor. I got a gun. I wanted to find the guy who got her pregnant, and I wanted to hurt him, kill him."

"Oh Dad, no."

Reggie takes Bella's hands and shakes his head.

"No, no, no," he says. "I didn't do that. I didn't do anything like that. I never found the guy, not for certain. But I was going to leave you, the both of you. I was going to, but I didn't. I tried to make it work with your mother. And we sort of did.

We made it work sort of, and then she died. But all the while, I loved you. I always loved you. And I still love you. And I'm old now. And you're all I have."

"So," she says, "the thing with the Ectoscope™?"

"It'll show you everything. What happened between me and your mother. What happened between your mother and your real father, your real dad. Who he is. Where he is."

Bella thinks she should say something comforting to Reggie. She thinks she should tell him that it's really okay. That he won't lose her. That she doesn't care about some hypothetical real father. That he's her real father, the only father she's ever known. She thinks about Jesus and Simon Peter. She thinks she should say what she thinks Jesus would say, that there's nothing to be embarrassed about. That the truth will set them free. That everything coming to light is all for the better. She should say something generous and forgiving. But Bella doesn't feel generous or forgiving. She feels mostly blank and then confused. And then underneath that, probably angry, though she isn't sure.

Reggie looks at her. She knows him. She can tell he really needs her to say something. His eyes are getting desperate. He needs her to say something nice. But even something mean would be better than this silence. She breathes audibly. She rolls her eyes upward in an effort to keep from crying. She's not sure why she feels like crying. She's not sad.

On the Ectoscope™ Screen, Bella scrolls quickly through the history stuff, then switches to her saved programs, family stuff. She scrolls through that quickly as well, sort of looking for new renderings, sort of looking for what Reggie had talked about: his fights with her mother, and also the other thing.

She looks for those scenes, but not really, not intently. And either way, nothing new turns up. Instead, it's the scenes she's already seen and saved, birthday parties, awkward first dates, church services in the park, beach days. So many beach days. All personal stuff from her own life, curated for her off the timeline by the Ectoscope™ algorithm.

Bella slows the feed scroll, letting the previews start for some of them, before clicking through. Then she stops at one, not playing it, but not skipping it right away. The rendering is of her mother's one-year deathday. Bella is leaving her apartment. Reggie is outside. He has a box with him with mementos from her mother's life. The two of them stand and talk for a long time. Bella periodically looks through the box. The two of them go for a walk. Reggie carries the box the whole time. Then finally, they go to a pizza shop, and Reggie puts the box down on the patio table as they eat.

Bella then clicks over a couple scenes. She sort of has an idea what she's looking for. She stops at a rendering of Lake Tahoe. Again, Reggie is there too. They're on a fishing boat. They fish for a long time. They don't catch anything. They get off the boat. They go hiking. It's a long hike. All the while, they don't talk.

Bella leaves it on this for a while. She just sits and watches it, her and Reggie walking through the woods. She turns to Reggie. Reggie is watching too.

The context is not part of the rendering, but Bella remembers the day of this scene. It is her summer after graduate school. She's trying to decide if she really wants to marry her boyfriend at the time, this guy named Guy, a rich guy she met at church. And she can't understand why she's so sad even though he seems so great. Reggie takes her on this trip to Tahoe, and he just hangs out with her, not pushing her either way, until she's ready to talk about it, and she decides that Guy really isn't the guy for her, and Reggie says that he'd known all along, but also knew that Bella needed to come to that conclusion on her own, and anyway, he trusted her to figure it out. That all she needed was some space.

It's not in the rendering, not this stuff, not what they talked about or how she felt about it. Those parts are just in her head.

She turns again to Reggie, who's quiet still.

She asks, "Do you remember this, Dad? Do you remember?"

BIOGRAPHICAL NOTE

Pete Hsu is a Taiwanese American writer based in Pasadena, CA. He is the author of the experimental chapbook, *There is a Man* (Tolsun Books). His work has also been featured in several journals and anthologies, including Asian American Writers' Workshop's *The Margins*, *F(r)iction*, *The Los Angeles Review*, and *Los Angeles Review of Books*. He was a 2017 PEN Center USA Emerging Voices Fellow as well as the 2017 PEN in the Community Writer in Residence.

CPSIA information can be obtained
at www.ICGtesting.com
Printed in the USA
LVHW110425090922
727917LV00005B/6

9 781636 280530